"So th

Captain collapsed,

Mara said quietly, as if the information was not a matter of life or death, but only something out of which casual conversation could be made. "She turned to the page needed to make the second course correction and found that it was missing."

Giles turned sharply.

"Don't assume . . ." he began, but she cut him off.

"That means," she said, "that the second course change was never made; and, far from being headed for planet 20B–40, we aren't even headed for Belben.

"We're headed for nowhere."

"A good story well told, with some food for thought."
—Poul Anderson

"The authors combine wry speculation on class prejudices with exciting space opera in a very entertaining tale."
—Publishers Weekly

HARRY HARRISON AND GORDON R. DICKSON

THE LIFESHIP

A TIMESCAPE BOOK
PUBLISHED BY POCKET BOOKS NEW YORK

A Timescape Book published by
POCKET BOOKS, a Simon & Schuster division of
GULF & WESTERN CORPORATION
1230 Avenue of the Americas, New York, N.Y. 10020

Published by arrangement with Harper & Row Publishers, Inc.
Library of Congress Catalog Card Number: 75-25079

ISBN: 0-671-42427-0

First Pocket Books printing June, 1977

10 9 8 7 6 5 4 3 2

POCKET and colophon are trademarks of Simon & Schuster.

Printed in the U.S.A.

THE
LIFESHIP

The explosion drummed and shuddered all through the fabric of the Albenareth spaceship, just as Giles reached the foot of the ladder leading up from the baggage area into passenger territory. He grabbed the railing of the spiral staircase that was the ladder and hung on. But almost on the heels of the first tremor came an unexpected second explosion that tore him loose and threw him against the further wall of the corridor, smashing him into the metal surface.

Stunned, he stumbled back to his feet. He began to pull himself up the staircase as fast as he could, gaining speed as he went. His mind cleared. He could not have been unconscious for more than a few seconds, he thought. At the top of the stairs he turned hastily back down an upper corridor toward the stern and his own stateroom. But this wider, passenger corridor was already filling with obstacles in the shape of bewildered, small, gray-suited men and women—arbites indent to Belben; and abruptly the loud and terrible moaning of an emergency, ship-out-of-control signal erupted into life and continued without pause. Already the atmosphere of the corridor had the acrid taste of smoke, and there were cries to him for help from the half-seen figures of the arbites.

The incredible was happening. Below them and around them all, the great spaceship had evidently caught fire from the two explosions, and was now helpless, a brief new star falling through the endless distances of interstellar space. Spaceships were not supposed to burn, especially the massive vessels of the Albenareth—but this one was doing so.

A coldness began to form in the pit of Giles' stomach; for the air around him was already warming and now beginning to haze with the smoke, and the sounds of arbite terror he heard tore at his conscience like sharp and jagged icicles.

He fought off his ingrained response toward the frightened indentees around him, walling it off, surrounding it with his own fury. He had a job to do, a duty to finish. That came first, before anyone or anything. The arbites aboard were not his direct responsibility. He began to run, dodging the hands of the reaching figures that loomed up through the smoke ahead of him, brushing them aside, now and then hurdling a fallen one who could not be side-stepped.

And all the while around the cold core in him, his fury grew. He put on speed. Now there was occasional debris in the corridor; here and there, panels in the walls, glimpsed through the smoke, sagged away from him like sheets of melting wax. None of this should be happening. There was no reason for wholesale disaster. But he had no time now to figure out what had gone wrong. The moans and cries of the arbite passengers still tore at him, but he plunged on.

A darker, narrower-than-human figure loomed suddenly out of the smoke before him. A long, oddly boned hand, a three-fingered hand, caught his bright-orange shipsuit and held him.

"To a lifeship!" brayed the Albenareth crewman, almost buzzing the human words. "Turn about. Go forward! Not to the stern."

Giles checked his instinct to surge against the restraining hand. He was large and powerful, stronger by far than any arbite, except those bred and trained to special uses; but he knew better than to try to pull loose from the apparently skinny fingers holding him.

"My Honor!" he shouted at the alien, using the first words he could think of to which an Albenareth mind might respond. "Duty—my obligation! I'm *Steel*—Giles *Steel* Ashad, an Adelman! The only Adelman aboard here. Don't you recognize me?"

The alien and he were trapped in a moment of motionlessness. The dark, lipless, narrow face stared into his from inches away. Then the hand of the Albenareth let go and the alien mouth opened in the dry crackling laughter that meant many things, but not humor.

"Go!" said the crewman. Giles turned and ran on.

Just a little farther brought him to the door of his suite. The metal handle burned his fingers and he let go. He kicked the door with a grunt of effort, and it burst open. Within, the bitter taste of thick smoke took him solidly by the throat.

He groped his way to his travel bag, jerked it open, and pulled out the metal box inside it. Coughing, he punched out the combination, and the lock of the box let go, the lid sprang open. Hastily he pawed through the mass of papers within. His fingers closed on the warrant for extradition, crammed it into a suit pocket, and dipped down to rip open the destruct trigger that would incinerate the box with all the rest of its contents. A white-hot flare shot up before him and the metal frame of the container collapsed like melting ice. He turned, hesitated, and pulled tools from inside his shipsuit. He had meant to hide these carefully, once his job was done; but there was no point in hiding anything now. Still coughing, he tossed the tools into the heat of the still-flaring container, turned, and plunged once more into the clearer air of the corridor, heading back finally toward the bow of the vessel and the particular lifeship he had been assigned to.

The Albenareth crewman was gone from his post when Giles passed that point again. Under the ceiling lights, the corridor was misty with smoke, but free now even of the figures of arbites. A small hope flickered in him. Perhaps someone else had taken charge of them by this time. He ran on. He was almost to the lifeship. There were voices in conversation just ahead—then something large and dark seemed to flicker up in front of him, out of nowhere, and something else that felt like a giant flyswatter slapped him from his feet.

He was momentarily staggered, but recovering even as he fell backward to the soft surface of the corridor. His head clearing, he lay for a second fighting to stay conscious. Now that he was down where the smoke was thinner, he could see that he had run into a door someone had left standing open. As he lay there, he heard two arbite voices—one male, one young and female—talking.

"You heard that? The ship's breaking up," the man said.

"There's no point our waiting out here now. The lifeship's just down that short hall. Let's go."

"No, Mara. Wait . . . we were supposed to wait . . ." The man's voice trailed off.

"What're you afraid of, Groce?" The girl's voice had an edge to it. "You act as if you don't dare breathe without permission from her! Do you want to stay here and choke to death?"

"It's all right for you . . ." muttered the male voice. "I've never been mixed up in anything. My record's perfect."

"If you think that matters—"

Giles' head was clear now. He rolled to his feet in one quick motion, stepped around the open door, and joined the two smaller gray-suited figures beyond it.

"All right," he said, crisply. "You're correct, girl. The lifeship's just down the corridor, here. You—what's your name? Groce? Lead off!"

The male arbite turned without a word and obeyed, responding instinctively to the note of command he would have heard from Adelborn all the days of his life. He was a short, round-headed, stocky man in early middle age. For a second, before following, Giles glanced curiously at the girl arbite. She was small, as all those of the lower class were, but good-looking for an arbite. Under her light-brown, close-cropped hair, her pale, narrow face was composed and unafraid. No doubt some high-caste blood in her ancestry somewhere, Giles thought.

"Good girl," he said more gently. "You follow me, now. Hang on to my jacket if the smoke gets too thick to see."

He patted her on the head before stepping out in front of her. He had turned away and did not see the sudden wild flash of indignation and anger that twisted her features as his hand touched her head. But the look was gone almost as soon as it had appeared. She followed him with the normal calmness of arbite expression on her face.

Giles reached out ahead to close his hand on the right shoulder of Groce. The man flinched at the touch.

"Steady, there!" snapped Giles. "All you have to do is obey. Move, now!"

"Yes, Honor," muttered Groce, doubtfully. But his shoulder squared under Giles' fingers. His step became firmer, and he led the way into the smoky corridor.

The smoke thickened. They all coughed. Giles felt the

hand of the girl, Mara, grope for the slack of his jacket in back and take hold of it.

"Keep moving!" said Giles, between coughs. "It can't be much further."

Suddenly they came up against a barrier.

"A door," said Groce.

"Open it. Go on through!" snapped Giles, impatiently. The arbite obeyed—and suddenly they were all in a small area where the smoke was less dense. Mara pushed closed behind them the door by which they had just entered.

There was another door directly in front of them, also closed. A heavy airlock door. Stepping past Groce, Giles pushed at it without being able to open it, then pounded on its activating button with his fist. The door opened slowly, swinging inward, away from them. Beyond was an airlock space and a further airlock door, open.

"Go," said Giles briefly to the two arbites, pointing to the other open lock. Mara obeyed, but Groce hesitated.

"Honor, sir?" he asked. "Please—what happened to the spaceliner?"

"An explosion somewhere aft. I don't know what caused it," answered Giles, shortly. "Go ahead, now. The lifeship's through the further lock, there."

Groce still hesitated.

"What if there's others coming?" he asked.

"Anyone coming will be here soon," Giles said. "With this smoke already in the corridors, there isn't much time. This lifeship is going to have to be launched soon."

"But what if, when I get inside—"

"When you get inside," Giles said, "there'll be an Albenareth there to tell you what to do. There's an alien officer in charge of any lifeship. Now, *move!*"

Groce went. Giles turned back to make sure that the airlock door behind him was closed. The smoke was eddying around him, although he could not see the source of the air current that was moving it, now that the shipside airlock door was closed. A loudspeaker over the closed door echoed suddenly to the sound of distant coughing.

"Sir," said the voice of Groce, unexpectedly behind him, "there isn't any Albenareth in the lifeship yet."

"Get back inside. Wait there!" he snapped at the arbite, without turning his head. The sound of coughing from the loudspeaker was louder now, echoed by the clang of stumbling feet approaching. One of those coming, Giles thought, had better be the Albenareth officer. Giles could pilot his own yacht around the Solar System, but as for handling an alien lifeship . . .

He punched the "open" button. The inner lock door swung wide. Dim figures were stumbling toward him in the smoke. Giles swore. They were all human, dressed alike in the dusty gray of their arbite shipsuits. There were five of them, he counted as they came closer, clinging to one another's clothing, several of them whimpering when they were not coughing. The one in front was an angular, gray-haired woman who dipped her head briefly in an automatic gesture of respect when she saw him. He opened the inner door and motioned them inside, moving aside so they would not brush against him as they went. Before the last one was in, the corridor lights flickered, went out, came back on again—then died completely.

Giles closed the door behind the five and touched the glow button on his watch. Under normal conditions the light from the dial was normally quite strong, but now it only lit up the rolling smoke, let in from the corridor. The air holding the smoke was hotter too; the fire could not be far away. He was coughing again, and could not control it, his head aching from the fumes.

With a sharp clang a section of the airlock wall fell away and Giles turned in that direction. The air current from a hidden source was suddenly stronger, and there was an elongated opening in what had appeared to be solid metal. The smoke was being sucked into it strongly. In the partially clear air a tall, thin form appeared, stooping with its head to pass through the opening.

"About time!" Giles said, coughing. The Albenareth did not answer him, moving quickly in a typical broken-kneed gait to the lock, with Giles close behind. Once they were both inside, the Albenareth turned and dogged shut the inner lock door. The action spoke for itself; the clash of the dogged lock echoed on Giles' ears like the closing of a coffin lid.

The voices of the arbites had dropped into silence as the Albenareth and Giles entered, and those already there moved warily aside from the alien. Still silent, the gaunt figure reached down into a slot in the soft flooring and pulled up a metal frame laced with flexible plastic. It was an acceleration cot, and a good deal of dust came up with it.

"Open the cots like this," the Albenareth ordered, the human words coming out at last, high-pitched and buzzing. "Strap down. Motions will be abrupt."

In the continuing silence, he turned and strode to the control console in the lifeship's nose, and belted himself into one of the two control chairs there. His three-fingered hands moved swiftly. Lights glowed on the panels and the two viewscreens before him came to life, showing only the out-of-focus metal walls of the lifeship capsule. Giles and the arbites aboard had just enough time to pull up their cots before the launch button was hit. They clutched at the frames of their cots as the sudden acceleration pounced on them.

Explosive charges blew away the hull section covering the lifeship capsule. Gravity forces pressed them hard against the webbing of their cots, as the lifeship was hurled away from its mother ship, into space. The acceleration changed direction as the lifeship's drive took over and moved it away from the dying ship; and a nauseating sensation rippled through their bodies as they left the gravity field of the larger vessel and the weaker grav-simulation field of the lifeship came on.

Giles was aware of all this only absently. Automatically his hands were locked tightly about the metal frame of his cot to keep him from being thrown off it, but his eyes were fixed on the right of the two viewscreens in the bow. The screen on the left showed only stars, but the right-hand screen gave a view directly astern, a view filled with the image of the burning, dying ship.

There was no relation between the jumble of wreckage seen there and the ship they had boarded in orbit high above the equator of Earth, twelve days before. Twisted and torn metal glowed white-hot in the darkness of space. Some lights still showed in sections of the hull, but most of it was dark. The glowing wreckage had shrunk to the size of a hot ember as they hurtled away from it; now it maintained a constant size and moved from screen to screen as they orbited about it. The Albenareth that had joined them was speaking into a grille below one of the screens, in the throbbing buzz of his own tongue. He or she was pronouncing what were clearly the same words, over and over again, until there was a scratching hiss from the speaker and another voice answered. There was a rapid discussion as the burning wreck was centered on the forward screen, then began to grow in size once more.

"We're going back!" an arbite voice shouted hysterically from the darkness. "Stop him! We're going back!"

"Be quiet!" Giles said, automatically. "All of you—that's an order!" After a second, he added, "The Albenareth knows what has to be done. No one else can pilot this ship."

In silence the arbites continued to watch as the image of the wreckage grew before them, enlarging until it filled the screen—until it appeared they were driving down into it. But the smooth play of the Albenareth's six long fingers on the control console keys controlled the lifeship's motion, sent it drifting inward, slipping past jagged fangs of steel that swam into view in the lifeship's forward viewscreen. Suddenly, there was a smooth, unscarred section of hull before them and they clanged against it. Magnetic clamps thudded as they locked on, and the lifeship was moved spasmodically, with loud grating sounds, as it was oriented with something on the hull. Then the alien rose from the controls, turned, and strode back to undog the airlock. The inner door ground open—then the outer one.

There was no rush of air, for they were sealed tight to another airlock—one on the spaceliner. The outer door of this lock, chilled from space and white-frosted with condensation, opened a crack, then stopped. The Albenareth wrapped a fold of his smocklike garment around his hands, seized the open edge, and pulled strongly until it opened all the way. Smoke haze beyond it cleared briefly to reveal another airlock and the gaunt figures of two more Albenareth.

There was a rapid conversation between the three aliens. Giles could make out no expression on the creased and wrinkled dark skin of their faces. Their eyes were round and unreadable. They punctuated their words with snapping gestures of their three-fingered hands, opening and closing the mutually opposed fingers. Suddenly, their talk ceased. Both the first Albenareth and one of the others reached out to touch the fingertips of both their hands, briefly, with those of the third, who stood deepest within the lock.

The two closer aliens stepped back into the lifeship. The one they left did not move or try to follow them. Then, as the airlock door began to close, all three began to laugh at once, together, in their high-pitched clattering laughter, until the closing door separated them. Even then, the captain and the alien beside him continued to laugh as the lifeship moved away from their shipmate in the spaceliner wreckage. Only slowly did their laughter die, surrounded by the staring silence of the arbite passengers.

Shock at the sudden disaster, fatigue, and smoke inhalation, or perhaps all these things, combined to numb the watching humans as they stared with reddened eyes at the image of the burning ship, pictured on the sternview screen in the front of the lifeship. The image dwindled, until it was no more than a star among all the other points of light on the screen.

Finally, it winked from sight. When it was gone, the tall alien who had first entered the lifeship and driven it outward from the spaceliner rose from the control seat, turned, and came back to face the humans, leaving the other alien doing some incomprehensible work with part of the control panel. The first Albenareth halted an arm's length from Giles, and raised one long, dark finger, the middle of the three on his hand.

"I am Captain Rayumung." The finger moved around to point back at the second alien. "Engineer Munghanf."

Giles nodded in acknowledgment.

"You are their leader?" demanded the Captain.

"I am an Adelman," said Giles, frigidly. Even allowing for the natural ignorance of the alien, it was hard to endure an assumption that he might be merely one of a group of arbites.

The Captain turned away. As if this action were a signal, a number of voices called out from among the arbites —all of which the Captain ignored. The voices died away

16

as the tall form returned to the control area and from
a compartment there took out a rectangular object wrapped
in golden cloth, and held it ceremoniously at arm's length
for one still moment before putting it down on a hori-
zontal surface of the control panel. The Engineer moved
to stand alongside, as the Captain put one finger on the
surface of the cloth. Both then bent their heads in silence above it, motionless.

"What is it?" asked the voice of Groce, behind Giles.
"What's that they've got?"

"Be quiet," said Giles, sharply. "It's their sacred book
—the Albenareth astrogational starbook holding their navigation tables and information."

Groce fell silent. But the determined voice of Mara,
ignoring his order, took up the questioning.

"Honor, sir," she said in Giles' ear. "Will you tell us
what's happening, please?"

Giles shook his head, and put his finger to his lips, refus-
ing to answer until the two aliens had raised their heads
and begun to unwrap the golden cloth from about their
book. Revealed, it was like something out of the human
past—as it was indeed out of the Albenareth past—a thing
of animal-skin binding and pages of a paper made from
vegetable pulp.

"All right," said Giles at last, turning around to find
the arbite girl right behind him. He spoke to her and to
all the rest as well. "Spacegoing and religion are one and
the same thing to the Albenareth. Everything they do to
navigate this lifeship or any other space vessel is a holy
and ritual act. You should all have been briefed about that
when you were sent to board the spaceliner, back on Earth."

"They told us that much, sir," said Mara. "But they
didn't explain how it worked, or why."

Giles looked at her with a touch of irritation. It was
not his duty to be tutor to a handful of arbites. Then he
relented. It would probably be better if they were informed.
They would all be living in close quarters under harsh
conditions for some days, or even weeks. They would
adapt better to their privations if they understood.

"All right. Listen, then, all of you," he said, speaking
to them all. "The Albenareth think of space as if it were
heaven. To them, the planets and all inhabited solid
bodies are the abode of the Imperfect. An Albenareth gains

Perfection by going into space. The more trips and the more time spent away from planetfall, the more Perfection gained. You noticed the Captain identified himself as 'Rayumung' and the Engineer as 'Munghanf.' Those aren't names. They're ranks, like stair-steps on the climb to a status of Perfection. They've got nothing to do with the individual's duties aboard a space vessel, except that the more responsible duties go to those of higher rank, generally."

"But what do the ranks mean, then?" It was Mara again. Giles gave her a brief smile.

"The ranks stand for the number of trips they've made into space, and the time spent in space. There's more to it than that. The rougher the duty they pull, the greater the count of the time involved toward a higher rank. For example, this lifeship duty is going to gain a lot of points for this Captain and Engineer—not because they're saving our lives, though, but because to save us they had to pass up the chance to die in the spaceliner when it burned. You see, the last and greatest goal of a spacegoing Albenareth is to die, finally, in space."

"Then they won't care!" It was an abrupt cry, almost a wail, from someone else in the crowd, a dark-haired arbite girl as young as Mara, but without the marks of character on her face. "If anything goes wrong they'll just let us die, so they can die!"

"Certainly not!" said Giles sharply. "Get that idea out of your heads right now. Death is the greatest achievement possible to an Albenareth, but only after one of them has done his best to fulfill his duties in space for as many years as possible. It's only when there's no place else to turn that the Albenareth let death take them."

"But what if these two decide suddenly there's no place to turn, or something like that? They'll just go and die—"

"Stop that sort of talk!" snapped Giles. Suddenly he was tired of explaining, ashamed and disgusted for them all—for their immediate complaints, their open and unashamed display of fears, their lack of decent self-restraint and self-control, and their pasty faces which had obviously spent most of their lives indoors away from the sunlight. All that was lower-class about them rose in his throat to choke him.

"Be quiet, all of you," he said. "Get busy now and pick

out the cot you want, beside whoever you want for a neighbor while we're in this lifeship. The one you pick is the one you'll have to stick with for the rest of the time we're aboard. I'm not going to have arguments and fights over changing places. After I've looked the lifeship over I'll get your names and tell you how you're to act until we reach planetfall. Now, get busy!"

They all turned away immediately, without hesitation—except, perhaps, the girl Mara. It seemed to Giles that she paused for just a second before moving to obey, and this puzzled him. It was possible she was one of those unfortunate arbites who had been unnaturally pampered, petted, and brought up by some Adelman family to feel almost as if she was one of the upper classes. Arbites hand-raised—so to speak—in such a manner were always maladjusted in latter life. They had not acquired proper habits in their early, formative years and as adults were never able to adapt to social discipline in normal fashion. If that was the case, it was a pity. She had so much else to recommend her.

He turned away from the arbites, dismissing them from his mind, and began a closer examination of the lifeship. It bore little or no similarity to the luxuriously comfortable and highly automated private spacecraft he, like most of the Adelborn, had often piloted among the inner worlds of the Solar System.

"Sir . . ." It was a whisper behind him. "Do you know —are they females?"

Giles turned and saw that the whisperer was Groce. The man's face was white and sweating. Giles glanced back for a moment at the two aliens. The Albenareth were almost indistinguishable as far as sex went, and both served indiscriminately at duties aboard spacecraft—and everywhere else on the alien worlds, for that matter. But the extra length of the Captain's torso was a clue and the particular erectness of that officer's stance. She was a female. The Engineer was a male.

Giles looked back at the sick paleness of fear on Groce's face. Among the arbites there were a thousand horror stories about the behavior of Albenareth females under certain glandular conditions, not merely toward their own "males" but—arbite superstitions had it—toward any other intelligent male creature. The basis of all the tales was

the fact that the Albenareth "female"—the two sexes of
the aliens did not really correspond equivalently to human
male and *female*—when in estrus, required from the
"male" not merely the specific and minute fertilizing
organism he had produced for the egg she carried, but
the total genital area of "his" body. This she took complete
into her egg sac, where it became connected to her own
bloodstream, part of her own body, and a source of nourishment for the embryo during its period of intrauterine
growth.

The acquisition of the "male's" genital area, entirely
normal by Albenareth standards, in human terms repre-
sented a rather massive mutilation of the "male" by the
"female." It effectively desexed the male until his genital
area should grow back, which took about two years,
roughly, by Earth time—long enough for the single Albenareth offspring to be born and learn to travel with
comfort upright on its two legs. Human xenobiologists had
theorized that in prehistoric times the evolutionary principle behind the desexing of the Albenareth "male" had
been to ensure his protection and assistance to the particular "female" carrying his progeny, during the vulnerable
period before she and it were fully able to take care of
themselves.

But such sophisticated understanding of alien instincts,
thought Giles, would be beyond the comprehension of arbites whispering among themselves in dark corners. Groce,
evidently, had the human lower-class horror and fear of
what the alien "female" might do to him, specifically, under certain conditions of glandular excitation. And probably every other arbite male aboard would react the same
way if any of them suspected the Captain's sex.

"They're officers!" Giles snapped. "Do they look like
females to you?"

Relief flooded back into Groce's face.

"No, Honor. No, sir, of course not . . . thank you, sir.
Thank you very much."

He backed away. Giles turned from the man, back to
his examination of the lifeship. As he did so, however, it
occurred to him to wonder just what the effect would be
on the arbites if a breeding impulse should take command
of the pair of aliens on board before they made planetfall.
Of course, he had no idea under what conditions such an

impulse could be generated; he put worry about it out of his mind. For the moment things were under control and that was all he required. He concentrated on examining the lifeship.

3

It was little more than a cylinder in space.

The rear half of the cylinder was occupied by the warp drive and the fusion chamber that powered it. In the cylinder's nose was the control console and the three viewscreens. The remaining space, like a tube with a flat floor inside, was a little over twelve meters in length and four in diameter. The floor was of a purple, spongy material that was clumsy to walk upon but comfortable for sitting or lying. The collapsible cots they had occupied while blasting free of the spaceliner were concealed beneath that same spongy surface.

Overhead, a glaring band of blue-white lights stretched the length of the lifeship. These, Giles had learned before leaving Earth, in his studies of the Albenareth and their space vessels, were never turned off, even when the lifeship was not in use. The continuous light source was needed to assure the healthy growth of the *ib* vine that completely covered all the exposed surfaces from midway in the lifeship's length, right back to the stern. The vine was life to all the passengers, alien and human alike; for the stoma in its flat, reddish-green leaves produced oxygen. The golden, globular fruit, hanging like ornaments from long, thin stems, were the only source of nourishment available aboard. The trunk of the *ib* vine, as thick through as a man's leg, emerged from a coffinlike metal tank in the stern that contained the nutrient solution to nourish the plant. A dusty metal hatch cover on the tank covered the opening into which all food scraps and waste were put for recycling. A simple and workable system for survival, a closed cycle in which the sanitary conveniences aboard consisted of a basin under a cold-water faucet and a covered container beside the tank.

The arbite passengers were not yet aware of how these things would circumscribe their existences aboard this alien craft. As yet, they had scarcely examined the new environment into which they had been thrust. The shock of awareness would be profound when it came. They were not Adelmen or Adelwomen, who under these same conditions would have felt an inner duty to maintain their self-control and not to give way to unseemly fears or yield in any way to the situation, no matter how unendurable.

He should start out gently, Giles told himself. He turned and went back to the others, who had now sorted themselves out, each on the cot he or she had pulled up and would occupy until they made planetfall.

"All set?" he asked them.

There were nods of agreement. He stood, looking down at them, a head taller than any except the obvious workgang laborer individual in the very rear. The others would tend to ostracize the laborer, he reminded himself automatically, as being even of lower class than themselves. He must not let that cause divisions among them while they were aboard here.

The laborer was as tall as Giles and doubtless outweighed him by twenty kilos. Outside of that, there was no resemblance. Only Giles, of all the humans there, showed the tanned skin, the handsome regular features, and the green eyes, with sun-wrinkles showing at the corners of them, that testified to both breeding and a lifetime of outdoor exercise. These differences alone would have set him apart from the rest, even without the expensive, gleaming fabric of the burnt-orange shipsuit he wore, in contrast to the drab, loose-fitting, gray coveralls that were their garb. Alone, his features were enough to remind the others that it was his to command, theirs to obey.

"All right," he said. "I am Giles *Steel* Ashad. Now, one at a time, identify yourselves." He turned to Mara, who had taken the front cot space on his left. "You first, Mara."

"Mara 12911. I'm recop, on indent to Belben like the rest."

"All right." He turned to Groce on the right, across from Mara. "Next, we'll take them in this direction. Speak up, Groce. Give your name and specialty number."

"Groce 5313, indent for three years, computer control section, Belben Mines and Manufacture."

"Very good, Groce. Glad to see you kept your compute by you."

"Go no place without it, sir. Feel naked without it."

Giles saw several of the others smile at this time-worn joke. Computecoms were always supposed to be unable to think without making a calculation first. This was good; a feeling of order was being restored. The next man behind Groce was thin, blond, and wiry, his fingers nervously tapping out unheard rhythms on his thighs.

"Esteven 6786, entertaincom," he said, in a tenor voice. "I'm setting up the broadcast system to Belben, to replace the automated one there now."

"Yes. Is that a recorder in your wallet?"

"Yes, Honor, sir. Would you like to see it? A multiplex memory store for the music."

"Very good—we can use that for a log of this voyage."

Giles put out his hand. Esteven stepped forward, but hesitated for an instant before taking out the flat case.

"But you won't wanf to wipe all the music to record, will you, sir? Please? We'll find some entertainment welcome, here in this little ship. . . ."

Giles winced internally at the pleading note in the man's voice. Even an arbite should not have to beg like that.

"Not all of the music," said Giles, "don't worry. Pick an hour to wipe clear for me. That should be enough. If it's not, I'll ask you for more."

"An hour?" Esteven's face lit up. "Of course, sir. A single hour's really no problem, of course. This has a bit of everything. I can wipe some of the jazzpop or early-decade symphonies. Or there are lots of musical commercials . . ." Esteven smiled hopefully and the others laughed, and the laughter quickly dying away when they saw that Giles was not smiling with them. "Honor, sir, forgive—naturally, I don't mean that. A joke only. Here, an hour from the music; it's all set." He passed the recorder over quickly, his hand shaking ever so slightly.

"I'll put everyone's name into this; we'll need to keep

records." Giles spoke into a recorder the names and numbers told so far.

"Now just you four left."

"Biset 9482. Supervise, indent one year." She stood up straight, across from Esteven's space, when she said it—the tall, angular, gray-haired woman who had led the party of survivors to the lifeship. She was, thought Giles, obviously used to authority. A lifetime had adjusted her to it—unlike the girl Mara. The two arbites side by side behind her were a dark-haired young man and an equally dark-haired plump girl. They had been holding hands until the others looked at them. The girl blushed; the man spoke for them both.

"Frenco 5022. This is my . . . wife, Di 3579. We're both comserv, indent seven years."

"Both just out of school, only on your first indent—and married already?"

The laughter of the others—free and open, this time—released a good deal of the tension that had been gripping them all. Frenco nodded and smiled and Di smiled, looking about, seeming to enjoy the sudden attention. She was the girl who had panicked when Giles spoke of the Albernareth seeking death, as a final act in space. Giles spoke their names into the recorder and looked beyond to the big laborer.

"Now you, lad."

The laborer touched his index and second finger to his forehead just below the cap of short-cut black hair, in a sort of half salute before answering.

"Hem 7624, Honor, sir," he said. His face was square and young, unwrinkled, but his voice had the rough and broken hoarseness of an aging person. "Graded manual, no specific skills, sir. But perfect work record."

"Good for you," said Giles. "We're lucky to have someone like you aboard, Hem, in case we have something to do that takes someone with strength we can rely on." He ran his gaze deliberately around the faces of the other arbites and saw that they had caught the social implication of his words. A couple of them flushed, and some of the rest looked sourly down at the floor. The girl Mara, however, was not one of them. Clearly they did not like Hem being placed on the same level as themselves, but they would put up with it.

Giles held the recorder. Esteven came and took it back.

"All right," Giles said. "Now, I'm going to talk to the Captain and see what information I can get. All I know at the moment is that either we ran into something or there was an explosion, and we seem to be the only ones who got out of the ship."

"Over two hundred people—human people—aboard, two hundred and twelve," Groce said hoarsely, tapping the figure into his compute as though to make it more real.

Giles shivered internally, feeling again within him the sharp teeth of conscience.

"And twelve alien crew members," he said loudly. "So we're the lucky ones. Just remember that, if things go badly. These lifeships are meant for survival and are a little short on comforts. You've seen how to work the cots. Those *ib* fruit you see on the vines are what we'll be eating, after the water has been pressed out of them. They're three-quarters fluid, so we'll have more than enough to drink. This plant's a mutation, gene-designed for this one function. Plenty of protein, so we're not going to starve."

"But, sir, how does it taste?" Di asked. Plainly, she had never eaten anything but prepared commissary food in her life.

"Is that . . . it?" the gray-haired woman named Biset asked, sniffing sternly as she pointed in the general direction of the covered pail.

"I'm afraid it is," Giles said. "But there should be folding partitions stored in the floor or walls here somewhere. I'll ask the Captain. We can arrange something for privacy."

"Ask him why we went back for that other pruney." Now that the fear was ebbing away, Groce was beginning to show anger. "We could've been killed, all of us!"

"The Captain had to have a good reason for acting as he did. I'll ask him what it was. But listen to me, everyone. None of you, obviously, have ever been in space before; but I know you'll have heard dozens of wild stories about the Albenareth. Forget those stories—now! We're all dependent on those two aliens up front, there, for our survival. So the term 'pruney' isn't to be used again by any of you. Is that understood? Now, check those cots of yours to see they're all in working order, and keep your voices down while I go and have a talk with the Captain."

Giles had been watching the two Albenareth as he talked. They had taken the starbook from its golden wrapping and placed it in its ritual, jewel-embossed clamp on the control console. Some plates had been removed from the sides of the console and the Engineer was probing delicately in the opening with the whisker-like prods of an instrument. The Captain sat silently, arms crossed, staring into the emptiness of space. Giles went and stood next to her.

"I would like to talk to the Rayumung," he said in buzzing Albenareth. The Captain slowly turned the glistening furrows of her face toward him.

"You speak our language."

"I am of the Steel sept. I go to space because this is what must be done. For the same reason I have learned your tongue. Please tell me what I need to know."

"My ship has been destroyed and I could not die with it. We will soon start and proceed to Belben."

"Belben?" echoed Giles.

"Belben," repeated the Captain.

"But how long will the voyage take?"

"I do not yet know exactly. Possibly a hundred shipdays. This small engine lacks efficiency, therefore the Munghanf is unlucky enough to be with us."

"It is his sorrow. Is the cause of the accident known?"

"There was no accident. My ship was destroyed by a deliberately caused explosion."

For the first time the Captain showed some sign of emotion, her voice raised, her fingers shaking.

"It's not possible," Giles began.

"There is no doubt. There were only empty cargo holds at the explosion site. Nor was there anything there that could burn. It would take nothing less than a fusion bomb to ignite the flooring, which burns only at the highest temperature."

Giles shifted his weight slightly on his feet.

"This is a grave charge," he said. *"Why would anyone want to sabotage an Albenareth spacer?"*

"That I do not know. But a crime has been committed." The dark alien eyes stared directly into Giles'. *"A crime one of my race would not commit."*

"There is no possibility the explosion was only an accident?" said Giles. *"Your ship was old, Rayumung. Many of the ships of the Albenareth are very old."*

"Their age is no matter. It was not an accident." The Captain's voice was unchanged, but her long, three-fingered

hands were now tightly clenched—a sign of deep emotion in an Albenareth, as Giles remembered from his studies of the aliens. He changed the subject.

"You said it would take possibly a hundred ship-days to reach Belben in this lifeship. Is there no destination closer?"

"Our destination was Belben. It is still Belben."

"Surely," said Giles, *"it would be more sensible to go to the closest point where safe planetfall is possible?"*

"I and my officers and my crew have fallen far back on the road to Perfection by permitting the loss of our ship." The dark eyes turned away from Giles, dismissing him. *"My Engineer and I may not even permit ourselves the redemption of death. To fail to reach our planned destination means a further loss of honor, and that is unthinkable. Farewell, therefore. Our talk is ended."*

Giles' temper twitched to life. He held it in check, and continued to talk in an even voice.

"I have not ended speaking, Rayumung," he said. The Captain turned her head back to face him. *"I have a responsibility for the other humans with me on board here. I make a formal request that you look for a closer destination that will shorten our time in this lifeship."*

The Captain stared at him a moment without speaking.

"Human," she said at last, *"we permit you to travel aboard our holy ships into holy space because you have no ships of your own worth the counting, and because it is a step upon the Way to assist others, even though they are aliens who will never know the meaning of Perfection. Also the rewards you bring us for carrying you permit more of our people than otherwise could to be unbound from the worlds of their beginnings. But you are only that which we carry of our own choice. You will not speak to me of destinations."*

Giles opened his mouth to answer, but the Captain's eyes had already looked past him, and she was talking again.

"Nor are you aboard this lifeship in such mode as I would prefer," she said. *"You are eight. The number is not optimum."*

Giles stared at her.

"I don't understand the Rayumung," he said.

"The number," repeated the Captain, *"is not optimum for Perfection in continuing our voyage to Belben. It would be more optimal if you were one less. Perhaps you will*

reduce your number by one individual." She pointed to the tank in the back of the lifeship. *"The converter could use the additional raw material."*

Giles stiffened.

"Murder an arbite, just to suit your idea of Perfection?" he snapped.

"Why not?" The dark, round eyes stared unblinkingly at him. *"You use them as slaves, but here in this small ship you have no need for so many slaves. What is one of them compared to the good will of myself, who hold survival of all of you in my hands? Why concern yourself for any of them?"*

A shock like the blow of some icy-bladed ax between his shoulder blades robbed Giles of words. It was several seconds before he could get himself under control enough to speak.

"They are arbites!" The buzzing Albernareth words lent themselves to being snarled by the human throat, and Giles heard himself snarling them. *"They are arbites, and I am an Adelman! An Adelman of a family who have been Adelborn for twenty generations! Put me in the converter, if you think you can, Rayumung. But lay one finger on any of these now under my protection, and I swear to you by the God of my race and the Perfection worshipped by yours that this lifeship will reach no destination at all, and you will die in dishonor, if I have to take the hull plates apart with my bare hands!"*

The Captain loomed over him. The wrinkled alien face, expressionless, was close to his.

"I suggested only, not commanded," said the Captain. A rare tone of emotion, of something almost like grim humor, crept into her voice. *"But do you really think you could match yourself against me, human?"*

She turned away. Giles found he was trembling like a dead leaf in the winter gale of his rage. He stood for a second until the shaking stopped, before turning around. It would not do to have the arbites see him otherwise than in perfect control of himself.

He had let himself react without thinking and the results had nearly been disastrous, to himself as well as to his mission. He should never have lost his temper. True, the destruction of another human being was nowhere near the small thing the Albernareth Captain thought it to be. But theoretically, Giles' duty was more important than every

arbite on this boat, and logic dictated that he should have
not hesitated to sacrifice one of them if his mission demanded it. Moreover, no doubt there were many of the
other Adelborn in the Oca Front who would never have
so hesitated. Still, he knew in his innermost self that if he
were to face that same suggestion from the Captain all
over again, his reaction would be no different.

He was a *Steel*—one of the ancient and honorable family who still lived and worked with the metal that had
given them their wealth and rank—unlike *Copper* or
Comsats or *Utl*, families who long ago had left the sources
of their names to the handling of their arbites. The metal,
steel, had lifted man on the first steps of his road to civilization. The Eiffel Tower and the San-Fran Bridge still
stood as monuments to the lifting. No one of the *Steel*
sept could in honor stand idly by and see a defenseless
arbite abused—let alone killed.

He calmed, inwardly as well as outwardly. There was
no question about his duty. He had only to follow his instincts—let live or die who might.

He turned back at last to the arbites with a face that
was composed and even smiling a little.

The panels for the partitions were dry and old like
much of the rest of the lifeship parts. Their fabric had
torn in Hem's thick fists as the large arbite pulled them
from their niches in the floor of the ship. Giles lay on his
cot, watching Groce and Esteven painstakingly gluing the
torn edges together with an adhesive film extruded by a
tool in the small repair kit the Albenareth Engineer had
been able to provide. The two aliens were supplied with a
permanent in-place screen behind their seats in the control
area, that they needed only to roll down and fasten. They
had been out of the sight of their human passengers most
of the time since they had done so, and for that bit of
screening, particularly, Giles was thankful. The less the
arbites saw of the aliens, he reasoned, the more likely they
would be to live with the Albenareth in harmony. Once
their own screens were repaired and in position, he would
set a couple of the women to harvesting the fruit of the *ib*
vine. But for the moment, work space aboard was too
crowded, with the panels spread out as they were for repair.

He transferred his gaze from his fellow passengers to the
ceiling of the craft, with its sections of utilitarian gray
metal. A far cry from the comforts of his own interplanetary yacht. . . . His mind drifted off to large problems,
the whole of his mission.

He had saved the warrant, thankfully. Without the
warrant, he would have to risk an assassination on a Col-

ony World where the police methods of those there would be unfamiliar. He smiled a little bitterly to himself. Once there had been no need for the Adelborn to kill one another, but Paul Oca had forced the chain of events that now moved to destroy him. If Paul had only been content to be their namesake, their philosopher, who had set them —all the conscientious young men and women of the Adelborn who had formed the Oca Front six years ago— on the road to cleansing and reawakening the human spirit. But some twist in Paul, some instinct to destruction, had pushed him to go one step further to suggest they throw open the doors of the Free Teaching Centers to the arbites, immediately.

"Are you insane, Paul?" Giles had asked.

"That's a ridiculous question," said Paul coldly.

"Is it?" said Giles. "You have to know that doing it suddenly would cause chaos—people starving in the streets in the long run, all governmental control broken down and production at a halt. Something like that has to be done step by step. Why do you think the world was put under the present social structure by our ancestors? There simply wasn't room enough or production enough to support the population and the power demands of an emerging technology. There wasn't any choice. Everybody realized that. It was time to stop developing civilization—all the wild growth in population and invention—for as long as it was necessary to get the race on a working basis, supporting itself without draining the planet any further. Now we've almost got to the point where the Adelman-arbite differences can be scrapped—and you want to smash everything that's been achieved by bringing in heaven immediately, fifty years ahead of schedule."

"I thought," said Paul—his white, regular features were unmoved from the classic impassivity and coldness of the Adelborn-schooled face—"you adhered to my principles of the Oca Front."

"I adhered, and I adhere," Giles said, "to the principle of what needs to be done. The Oca Front is made up of Adelborn, Paul. Remember that. I won't stand by for one member's ideas if I think they're wrong, any more than you would. Even when that member is you. You started the organization, Paul, but you don't own it. You're just one of a group that wants to work to bring this two-hundred-year-old, unnatural social structure to an end. If

you doubt that, check some of the other members for
opinions. You'll find they don't like your idea of revolution at this moment any more than I do. It smacks of
glory-hunting, wanting to have the skyrockets all go up in
your own particular time."

"Glory," said Paul, "hunting?" He made two words of it.

"I said that," said Giles, equally deliberately. Only
another Adelborn, looking at and listening to the two tall,
lean, level-voiced young men, would have realized that
they were on the verge of a deadly explosion. "I said that
and I meant that. As I say, check with others of the Front.
You'll find I'm not alone in my opinion."

Paul looked at him for a long second.

"Giles," he said, "I've doubted your opinion was wise
once or twice in the past. This now confirms that doubt.
You fail in your concept of duty, which is everything to
us. We're caretakers for the rest of the race until the situation and their own growth makes them ready to come
of age. That duty is paramount. If you had it fully in you,
you'd understand that it makes no difference if opening
the Teaching Centers now causes widespread breakdown,
starvation—or any other temporary upheaval. If the time
has come, the time has come. But you, Giles, have a flaw.
You are—and always were—partly a romantic. You worry
about people, not the great shift and flow of human
history."

"People are history," said Giles. His tone and attitude
were unchanged, but inside himself he was feeling a sort
of despair. The flare of anger toward Paul's unreasonable-
ness which he had felt a moment earlier had quickly
burned itself out, as quickly as it had sprung up. Adelborn
did not have friends, at least in the old sense of the word.
As Paul had said, duty was everything. But as far as it
could be said there was friendship, Paul had been his oldest
and closest friend. Their relationship went back to their
first young years in the Academy together. They had been
side by side in the long dining halls, the austere dormi-
tories, the cold classrooms, and the barren sports fields.
Together, they had been changed from children who remembered and longed for even the limited family closeness of the Adelborn, to members of a ruling class who
knew only that duty Paul talked about, and who needed
or wanted nothing and no one else.

From that time on they had lived, each self-sufficient

and isolated within himself, as complete and separate individuals without the weaknesses of any closeness with any other human being. It was necessary that they be so, that corruption and human frailty not be allowed to damage the rigid structure of the survival society that their ancestors had set up, to be maintained until there should be room enough, food enough, and future enough for the race as a whole to be free again.

As it was, no one was free. In essence, the arbites were slaves to the Adelborn; and the Adelborn were slaves to their duty—to that survival program laid out two centuries before. The Adelborn were not to question that plan until survival for the race was assured, and they were not to permit the arbites to question it.

All this was true. And perhaps it was true too, as Paul had said, that Giles was a romantic and his sense of duty had a flaw in it. But at the same time Paul was wrong about opening the Centers this soon. If he insisted on doing so, the others in the Front would have to stop him—which necessarily would mean destroying him. No Adelborn would turn aside from what he considered a correct action merely because of the weight of opposition, or from any fear of personal consequences. Giles did not want Paul destroyed. He had done too much that was good already. He was too useful to be wasted. Once more, Giles tried to reach the other man by argument.

"Already the arbite class has had bad cracks in it, Paul," he said. "You know that as well as I do. There's that Black Thursday group of wild-eyed revolutionaries. There are these gangs that are starting to roam around beating up other arbites for the kick of it. Particularly, beating up the laboring arbites, as if they were trophies to be taken—and the other arbites know as well as we do that the laborers are genetically tailored to be harmless outside of the friendly brawling among themselves in their barracks. Finally, there's the arbite bureaucracy that's evolved over two centuries while the best of them were becoming a sort of noncommissioned-officer class for Adelborn like us. Stop and think of those three groups, each with its own self-interest or blindness to the Survival Plan you and I have in our very bones. If you could throw open the Teaching Centers tomorrow, do you think the individuals of each of those arbite groups would sit back and wait to let the Plan accomplish itself? You know better.

You must know that each one would dive into the chaos caused by relaxation of the social order, to get the biggest possible slice of authority in the future for their own group's people. They'd tear the arbite class apart, Paul. They'd each pick up adherents and this scarred old world would see war, once more. War in the streets, with each man out to destroy his neighbors!"

Giles ran down. There was nothing much more he could say about the dangers of arbite reaction. He gazed at Paul hoping for a counterargument—anything to show that there was still hope of reaching him with logic. But there was no sign in Paul's face that he had been reached, not even the faint signs visible to a fellow Adelborn. Paul said only:

"Is that all you've got to tell me on the subject, Giles?"

"No," said Giles, with a sudden surge of feeling. "Not quite. There's the Albenareth to think of, too."

"The aliens aren't our concern," said Paul. "We didn't need them before the Plan was begun. They've been useful while it's been in operation because it was a great deal cheaper from a production standpoint to supply them with manufactured goods in payment of stellar transport than to build our own space fleet from scratch. With their help we've been able to develop new worlds for settlement at half the expense we'd have had otherwise. But now we'll be developing our own fleet anyway, so the Albenareth are no longer needed. In the future we can ignore them."

"No!" said Giles, grimly. "Our race can't just make contact with another race, use it for a couple of hundred years, and then walk away from it. If the Albenareth have been useful to us, we've been a lifesaver to them. Because our technology and labor force saved them work-hours their own people would otherwise have had to supply, they've come to put more of their people out in space than they can afford to support there, on their own. You've seen the private reports of the Council. Even with us supporting them, in recent decades—because space is such a religion with them—they've gone to the ragged edge of a survival economy in manning new vessels. To the point where they've got crews in spaceships that are dangerously undermaintained, or overage; and they aren't about to take such craft out of service, because no Albenareth is going to deny another Albenareth the chance to live and die in Holy Space."

"That's their concern," said Paul. "Let each race look to itself."

"It's our concern as well!" snapped Giles. "I tell you, words won't talk this away. It's no longer enough for the Plan to come up with a solution to our human problems. Any realistic solution has to take into account the Albenareth and their problems as well; for our sake as well as theirs, the Albenareth have got to come to terms with a religion that demands a life in space for every member of their race, but disregards the necessary planet-based economy sufficient to provide support for that life in space."

"I repeat," Paul said. "The Albenareth are no part of our problem. They can be ignored, to live or not live as they choose. Our only duty is to the survival of our own race. I think, no matter what you say, that the other members of the Oca Front will back me rather than you, on that."

He glanced across at the ancient, ornate grandfather clock that dominated the far wall of his study. It was the slightest of glances and his eyes came back immediately to Giles, but to another Adelborn the hint was more than sufficient.

"I'm sorry," said Giles, formally, getting to his feet, "if I've taken too much of your time; but I thought the subject was important. Perhaps we can talk more about it sometime soon."

"Perhaps," answered Paul. The single inflectionless word said "no" more plainly than any impassioned statement could have.

"In that case," said Giles, "I'll be talking to other members of the Front. One way or another, we'll find ourselves in contact, shortly."

"By all means," said Paul. "Good day."

"Good day."

Giles turned and went. Internally, as he left he was telling himself that he need not contact the other members right away. He could take a few days at least to think about Paul's attitude. Perhaps a miracle of persuasion could yet be worked.

But it was less than six weeks after their conversation that Paul disappeared; and less than another six months before his *Manifesto*, calling on all arbites to demand

Adelborn rights, had been found circulating among the lower class.

The search for Paul had been thorough, of course, after that. But within a week, Giles and others in the Oca Front were convinced—even if the World Police were not—that Paul Ocà was already off the Earth, and almost certainly out of the Solar System. Somehow, the arbites had helped him get away, possibly in a freight shipment to one of the frontier worlds.

To do so had taken organization. Which meant that some arbites at least had already begun to band together in revolutionary groups and think of the immediate burning of contracts and the unrestricted freedom of movement Paul had advocated to them.

So it was for a fact—the fact of arbite organization— that Paul Oca must die, once Giles had him. It would take willing, law-abiding arbites as well as duty-minded Adelborn to build the space fleet that must replace the alien ships. Lots of arbites and many Earth years. The genius-level intelligence of Paul Oca must not be allowed to lead and attempt an arbite revolution prematurely.

But it was not easy to kill an old acquaintance, Giles thought. Even if you knew that no matter how you hated killing him you would still go through with it when the time came, because an obligation to your duty had been built into you like an iron rod in place of a spine. . . .

The screens were reglued. One of the partitions reached almost across the cabin, making two separate rooms. The other, shorter partition enclosed the sanitary facilities, with its open end facing toward the rear of the craft for additional privacy. Giles got up from his cot.

"Mara, Di," he said, "come over here. You two are going to be in charge of picking the fruit."

"I never did that before." Di tried to hold back. Giles guessed her to be showing a common arbite fear of responsibility.

"I don't think it'll be too hard to learn," he said gently. "Come over here. Do you see the lower end of the stem on this fruit I'm pointing at? Twist the stem to break the fruit loose. Don't pull it off or you'll injure the vine. Collect about a dozen fruits apiece and bring them down here." He turned to look for the graded arbite. "Hem, how strong are you feeling today?"

Hem bounded to his feet from the cot on which he had stretched out. He grinned crookedly.

"No one ever beat me in the barracks, sir." Solid, scarred fists closed at the memory. "You show me what you want done, Honor, sir."

"Well, you don't have to fight anybody, not yet at least," Giles said easily. "Though I'm sure you're good at it. I've got something that calls for someone with good muscles."

"That's me!"

"All right, then. This is the fruit press." Giles pointed to a heavy cast-metal apparatus fixed to the wall. There was a round opening at the top and a long lever projected from the center; scuffed plastic containers were locked into position below it. "You lift the handle and drop the fruit in here, like this. Then, press down hard on the handle. The juice drains down on this side and, when you lift the handle, the two halves drop into the other container. Then you're ready to repeat the process."

"I can do that, easy!"

It did not actually take much effort to squeeze the fruit, but Hem threw himself into the operation with a will.

"Containers full, sir," he announced when he was done.

"Very good. Now who'll be the first to try this food?"

The truth was, Giles had to admit to himself, that the green-gold pulp looked repulsive. The arbites shied away. Giles smiled at them encouragingly, dipped a bowl into the stuff, and dug out a gobbet. There were no utensils of any kind aboard, so he had to use his fingers. The pulp was slimy and had a musty odor like worm-ridden wood. He popped a lump into his mouth and chewed industriously. Thankfully, it had almost no taste, but the texture was very unpleasant. The juice, however, was a good deal better. It was almost pure water with only an edge of sweetness to it. He held the bowl of pulp out and, after some hesitation, Di took a tiny bit. And instantly spat it out.

"Phoo! That's terrible."

"I don't think it's really that bad. I imagine we'll get used to it. Anyone else hungry?"

The only other taker was Hem. He chewed and swallowed without expression and finished a whole bowl. Apparently flavor, or the lack of it, made little difference to him.

"Stuff's all right," was all he said.

"One satisfied customer already," said Giles. "I'm not

going to force anyone, but the *ib* fruit is here. During the next twelve hours I want you all to try it. We're all going to stay in condition and no one's going to get sick. This is our food and we're going to eat it." To prove the point he filled the bowl again and managed to finish everything in it without changing expression. It is often easier to lead than to follow. He was rinsing his hands clean at the basin, not successfully because the water in the tank was *ib* fruit juice, when Mara approached him.

"Did the Captain say how long this trip will last?"

He had been braced for someone to ask him that. She deserved an answer.

"It's not going to be a short one," he said. "That I'm fairly sure of. As soon as the Captain has worked out the figures I'll let you all know."

"Did he say why they left that other crewman on the ship?"

Giles also had been waiting for someone to ask him this and had worked out what he thought was a satisfactory answer. There would certainly be trouble if the arbites discovered that the engines weren't functioning correctly.

"To understand the Albenareth you need to know something about their philosophy . . . their religion, or whatever you want to call it," he told her. "To them the mere act of being in space is a blessing. They gain what I suppose you'd call 'holiness' by being many years in space. About the only thing that exceeds the value of many years spent in space is the honor of dying there after a lifetime of service. So the ones that were left on the ship were fortunate by their standards—and that included the one of them that had a chance to go with us but stayed behind. From this point of view it was probably the most important and best thing that ever happened to him."

She frowned.

"That sounds, well, almost sick, doesn't it? I mean being in space is just being in space. Dying there certainly doesn't accomplish very much, either."

"Apparently the Albenareth think it does." He made an effort to bring the conversation back to the present. "Have you picked all the fruit we'll need?"

"A lot more than we need. Nobody's rushing to eat it. We had both baskets filled, and the bumper's been working up a sweat squashing them."

"Bumper?" He had never heard the term before.

She looked at him a little warily, then her tenseness of expression dissolved into a smile.

"Bumper . . ." she said. "It's a name for someone of the graded ranks. I can call Hem that, but you shouldn't."

"Why?"

"Because . . ." She hesitated. "Actually, it means someone who got dropped on his head when he was small, and who doesn't have all his brains because of it. Among . . . us, it's just a word. But if you used it, Hem would think you meant it literally."

He gazed at her curiously.

"You express yourself well," he said.

For a second he thought he saw something that might have been a flash of anger in her eyes. If so, however, it was gone before he could be sure it had been there at all.

"For an arbite, you mean," she said. Her voice was perfectly even and calm.

"Why, yes," he said. "I don't expect you to have had the advantages of a wide education."

"No, you wouldn't, would you?" she murmured. "I should thank you for the compliment, then."

"Compliment?" he said, bemused. A compliment was something you gave to an Adelwoman, not to a girl like this. "I was just stating a fact—a fact you should be proud of, of course."

"Oh, I am." There was a slight edge to her voice, but it changed abruptly. A note of sadness crept into it and she looked down at the spongy floor of the lifeship. "Along with the others, I'm glad just to be alive. When I stop to think about how many there are back on Earth who'd give anything they have to be out here in space, even if it meant being on this lifeship . . ."

He stared at her, puzzled.

"You mean there're arbites who like space travel that much?"

She shifted her face to look at him. For a second he thought she was going to laugh at him—an unpardonable breach of manners, of discipline, coming from someone like herself to an Adelborn.

"Of course not," Mara said. "I'm talking about the chance to indent to one of the Colony Worlds—a chance to get off Earth."

"To get off Earth?" The girl was a bundle of strange remarks. "To get away from a safe life on the Mother

World—away from the pleasure parks and the entertainment centers—and to go out to work for long hours with a restricted diet, and under harsh conditions? Why should an arbite want that?"

"Why should an Adelborn want it?" she said. "But many of the upper people do."

"But that's entirely different." He frowned. There was no way to explain to this child of the underclasses, with her no doubt permissive upbringing, what it was like to accept the self-discipline and singleness of purpose that were the duties of the Adelborn from the moment they were old enough to walk. Faintly, from very long ago, he remembered the loneliness of being four years old and separated from his family, sent to a boarding school to begin the training that would fit him for his adult responsibilities as a leader of the race. He had cried—he winced with shame now at the memory—that first night, silently into his pillow. Many of the other small Adelborn in his barracks had cried also their first night, but only one of them openly. The fact was that that one, a boy, had continued to cry, if more quietly, on succeeding nights, and at the end of the first week he was taken away. To where, the rest of them never discovered, for none of the masters or mistresses at the school would talk about him.

"That's different," Giles said again to Mara, now. "It's a matter of responsibility for our class, as you know. Adelborn don't go out to the Colony Worlds because they prefer it there to Earth. They go because duty points them that way."

She was watching him closely.

"You really believe that, don't you?" she said. "Haven't you ever done what you wanted—just because you wanted it?"

He laughed.

"Come, now, Mara," he said. "What sort of an Adelman would I be if I could say yes to a question like that?"

"A human one."

He shook his head at her, amused but completely baffled.

"Honor, sir," a voice spoke in his ear. He looked around and saw that Frenco had come in and was waiting to get his attention.

"What, Frenco?"

"The Captain wants to see you. He spoke to me in regular Basic and said to tell you."

The Captain had his fingertips resting on the book on the console before him when Giles stepped behind the controls partition. The Engineer stood stolidly at his side.

"You wished to talk with me?" Giles asked, in Albenareth.

"The Munghanf has located the problem in our drive."

"The Munghanf is exceedingly competent."

The Engineer touched two fingers together in the gesture that might be translated as meaning "your words give me pleasure," then he pointed to the engine compartment.

"Our power source operates well, the warp drive functions within the desired parameters. The malfunction is located in the radiant drive mounted on the hull outside. it must be repaired."

"Can it?" asked Giles.

"Most easily. There is a spacesuit here and I have the tools and knowledge to do what is needed."

"That is good." Giles nodded.

"It could be more than good. It could be of great reward for one person."

The Engineer picked up a bulky plastic bundle from the deck and pulled the spacesuit from it. The fabric crackled when he shook it out and held it up for Giles' inspection.

"Look here, and here, at the seams. They are stiff with age, cracking open. They could burst under internal pressure and leak air, and then whoever wears this suit may die in space. And it is I who must wear it if the necessary repairs are to be made!"

Before Giles could say anything more the Engineer was rocked by loud and continuous laughter.

5

Giles waited until the laughter died down. Then he spoke to the Engineer.

"*So the Munghanf approaches the further Portal of the Way,*" he said. "*My congratulations.*"

"*It is not certain yet,*" said the Engineer. He turned to look at the other dark, wrinkled alien face. "*Also, she has been my Captain through much time and space, and the I that is I would be lonely to go on without her. But as a passing from the suit failure would be an end result of the explosion that destroyed our vessel, my responsibility thereby would be canceled, and I cannot but hope.*"

"*The Munghanf has lived in duty and may properly proceed,*" said the Captain. "*But we will cease to talk of it now, Munghanf. The human can only look on this important thing that happens as through a thick wall of clouded transparency. The Way and its meaning are closed to his race.*"

"*That is so,*" said the Engineer, looking back at Giles. "*And at this moment I am sorry for it. Let my Captain speak.*"

"*I did not call you here on behalf of the Munghanf,*" said the Captain, addressing Giles. "*I will require your help. It must be the help of you, personally. I cannot trust this effort to one of your slaves.*"

"They are not," said Giles, speaking slowly and distinctly, "slaves. Mine, or anyone's."

"*They live to work and breed and die. I know no other*

43

term for such," said the Captain. "I will show you the work to be done."

She stepped past Giles and led him back to the inner door of the lifeship's airlock. To the left of it, the spongy wall covering had been peeled back to reveal a large panel, which the Captain pushed inward, then slid aside, to reveal a control console equipped with viewscreen and two hand-sized sockets just below it.

"Put your hands into the control openings," directed the Captain.

Giles stepped up to face the console and did so. Within the dark depths of the two sockets, his fingers found and closed over a pair of upright, movable rods, pivoted at their bottom end and each grooved to fit the three fingers of an Albenareth hand. In the depths of each groove was a stud that yielded to the pressure of Giles' grip.

The moment he touched the bars, the screen before him lit up and he saw a section of the outer hull from beyond two mechanical extensions ending in three metal fingers each. As he moved the bars and pressed harder on the spring-cushioned studs, the arms extended, waved one way or another, and the metal fingers flexed. Clearly what he had in his grasp was something mounted on the outer hull that was the alien equivalent of waldoes—mechanical hands operating in response to the movement of his own flesh-and-blood appendages upon the controls they grasped.

"I must stand by the general controls," the Captain said, "and put them in various modes as the Engineer works upon the drive. I am therefore needed at the main console while you will be here. From my position, I will be able to move the unit carrying the device with which your controls connect about the hull. But it will be up to you to operate it—if necessary, use it to carry the Engineer inside if he should fail before his work is done, or before he can return to the airlock under his own power."

"I will need to practice with these controls," said Giles. "I do not know them and they are not designed for my hands."

"There will be time for practice," the Captain said. "Preparations must be made. I will require the stern section of this vessel beyond your second screen, as space in which to set up necessary equipment. You must keep all humans out of that area until further notice."

"I'll take care of it," said Giles.

He turned, leaving the bow of the lifeship, and went back to the stern area behind the final screen the arbites had erected. This was a space containing the converter, the fruit press, and a good section of the *ib* vine. There were only two cots there—the cots of Frenco and Di. The young couple had been tacitly left with this place to themselves, to give them the closest approach to privacy that the lifeship afforded. It was an illusion of privacy, actually, for the screen was no barrier to sound, and the slightest movement or whisper could be heard beyond it by anyone who made it a point to listen.

The two young arbites were alone there when Giles arrived. They were seated facing each other, each on his own cot, holding hands and talking with their heads together in low voices.

"Frenco . . . Di," said Giles. "Forgive me, but I'm going to have to dispossess you for a little while. The Engineer has to go outside to work on the ship and this area's going to have to be used as back-up room for that effort. I'll let you in here again, as soon as it's available. Meanwhile, one of you can take my cot up front, and there's another cot across from it that's never been pulled up."

The two stood up, looking shy.

"Honor, sir," said Frenco. "How long is it going to be?"

"No longer than it has to," Giles said. "But that'll be a matter of hours. Why? Any particular problem?"

"It's just Di, sir," said Franco. "She's been having trouble sleeping—even back here alone with me. She has nightmares—she's always had nightmares—and she fights going to sleep. She can't help it. She probably won't be able to rest much at all, up front."

"I sympathize," said Giles. "But there's nothing I can do about it. If this was one of our own spacecraft, we'd have a medical kit on board and there'd probably be something I could give her to help her sleep. But it isn't, and I can't. I'll let you back here as soon as I can, though."

Defeated, Frenco and Di sidled out from between their two cots and started through the opening in the screen, obediently.

"And tell everyone else," said Giles, pitching his voice so that the flimsy screens would in no way block the other humans from hearing his message, "none of them are to so much as look back here until I tell them it's all right.

The Albenareth require complete privacy in this area, and I've promised it to them. So all our people are to stay clear. That's an order."

"Yes, Honor, sir," Frenco and Di chorused, disappearing.

They had scarcely gone when the alien Captain stepped through the opening and stood, looking around the area.

"No harm has been done here," she said to Giles in Albenareth. *"Good. The Engineer is busy with other preparations up front. I will prepare this space. You may go now. If I call you, you may come back."*

In spite of Giles' better judgment, her choice of expressions raised instinctive hackles of his temper.

"If you should ask my presence here," he retorted in icily correct Albenareth, *"my sence of duty would, of course, urge me to come."*

The dark, round alien eyes locked with his. There was absolutely no way of reading expression in them. Whether the Captain was angry, amused, or indifferent was beyond the power of Giles to tell.

"I will only call you if it is absolutely necessary," said the Captain. *"Go now."*

Giles left the stern arena and went back up to the airlock and the open control panel where he would be working. He slipped his hands into the two apertures, grasped the control rods, and began experimenting, practicing with them. It was clumsy work at first. The Albenareth waldo, like the Albenareth hand itself, had its three fingers all semi-opposed, so that their tips approached each other at equal angles of 120 degrees between them. They were not capable of being directly opposed in a straight line as the human thumb and forefinger are; and in spite of their normally greater strength, the clumsiness of any two fingers only in opposition made for a bad grip.

In the end, Giles taught himself to think of taking hold of anything at all in terms of a full-hand grasp. This concept brought all of his fingers into pressure on all three studs on any one of the control bars, and the result was closer to the Albenarethian.

He was practicing this attitude and reaction, when he felt a movement beside him and turned his head to see Biset standing beside him, as if waiting for his attention. He stopped what he was doing.

"Did you want to see me?" Giles asked.

"Please, Honor, sir," she said, "continue what you're doing."

She hesitated and abruptly switched languages, from Basic to the one she now named. *"I understand you speak Esperanto?"*

While she had been talking he had gone back to his practicing, and, because of the distraction of her sudden shift of tongues, he completely bungled the same three-fingered pickup he had been telling himself he now had almost under control. He exploded at her, reflexively, in the same tongue she herself had used.

"Cu, jes me bonege parloas Esperanto!"

He broke off and let go of the two rods, turning to look at her.

"How do you know that?" he demanded in Basic, lowering his voice. "It's an old international language. I got interested in it myself only five years ago. How did an arbite even come to hear about it?"

"Please, sir," she said, still in Esperanto, *"please continue working. It will be better if the others think that their lack of understanding is due to the noise, only."*

He went back to his practice with the waldoes.

"I asked you," he said, in Esperanto, *"how an arbite happens to know this particular old language—or in fact, anything but Basic? The earlier tongues of Earth are matters of academic study only, nowadays, unless you were born where one was spoken; and no particular territory owned Esperanto."*

"My case is special," she said.

He turned his head to look at her as he worked. Her thin, disapproving features were only inches away. As with the girl Mara, there were signs of some upper-class fineness of bone. This one must have had her share of good looks too, once.

"Yes," she went on, as if he had said out loud what he was thinking, *"I'm no common woman. I was raised in a good family. But that's something we can talk of at some other time. The important thing now is that you be told there is a member of the Black Thursday among us."*

Giles was suddenly, icily, alert. But he kept his hands moving on the rods; and before she could say more she was cut short by the sound of an Albenareth voice calling from the back of the lifeship in Basic.

"Human! Come now!"

Giles swung away from the control panel, his eyes still on Biset.

"Stay here," he said. "I'll talk to you later."

He went back through the gaps in the two screens, ignoring the questions and the somewhat frightened gazes of the arbites. He stepped into the stern area to find the Captain and the Engineer both there, the Engineer already wearing the spacesuit. On him, and semi-inflated up to the neck seal, it had become transparent enough to show his arms and legs clearly within the limbs of it. Helmetless, his head protruded from the neck seal like some dark seed being squeezed from a cluster of cloudy grapes.

"You are in command here," said Giles in Albenareth to the Captain. *"For that reason I overlook much in the name of our common necessities. Nonetheless, outright discourtesy on your part will be met with equal discourtesy on mine. When you speak the human tongue to me in front of other humans, you will use human courtesies, or I will not respond. I have a position to maintain as leader of this human group. Is that clear?"*

"Completely clear, O human of great honors," answered the Captain. *"I will call you 'Adelman' in future, especially whenever I speak to you in your own language. Now assist me—we must tie off this suit in places to ensure that the Engineer can continue working even if small leaks depressurize parts of it."*

She handed Giles what seemed to be short lengths of plastic cord with a metallic core—something partway between wire and rope. One end of each length had a small, odd-shaped clamp attached to it. The cords were long enough to go around the Engineer's spacesuited arm or leg two or three times before the clampless end was drawn through the clamp and so secured. In theory this binding and securing should have been a simple matter, but the weakness of the grav-simulation field aboard the lifeship made it not so. Work on the Engineer was done most efficiently when that alien was lying horizontally on one of the cots, but with both Giles and the Captain pushing and tugging at him, to wind or secure a cord about one of his limbs, his body bobbed or floated away into the air. In the end Giles' greatest usefulness, he found, was to hold the spacesuited alien figure as still as possible while the Captain worked with the cords.

When they were finished and the Engineer was once

more upright on his feet, holding himself in position like the rest with a hand on one of the hull or ceiling anchor points, he looked like a figure made out of very short lengths of fat link sausage, each tie compartmentalizing a section of his arm or leg. The ties were not so tight as to keep his suit's interior atmosphere from circulating, but in case of a leak, the sudden lack of pressure on the down side of a tie would cause the elastic material to clamp tightly enough to make a seal.

Or at least, thought Giles, gazing at the Engineer when they were done, that seemed to be the theory of the two aliens. But he could not really believe that the cord seals would be that efficient in case of spacesuit rupture. The thought came to him suddenly that perhaps this tying was only a ritual—merely a matter of going through some form of protecting the Engineer in a hopeless situation. Some such impractical gesture on the part of these members of a death-worshipping race might make sense to them. But still, thought Giles, it was odd.

"All right, Adelman," said the Captain. *"Come forward with us now. I will let the Engineer out the airlock, then move to the main controls. You will return to work your own console."*

They moved through the openings in the screens, past the stares of the arbites as the two of them helped the Engineer, now with his fishbowl helmet in place and completely sealed in the suit, to walk clumsily past.

The Captain punched the airlock controls, and the inner door of the lock swung open. Frost formed instantly on all surfaces within the lock now exposed to the interior warmth and atmosphere of the ship. The Captain wrapped plastic around his three-fingered hands to protect them from the icy metal surfaces, and set about connecting the umbilicals—the flexible tubes that would provide atmosphere, power, and heat—to the Engineer's suit.

At last it was done. The Captain stood back, and the inner lock door closed again. Without a further word to Giles, the alien turned and stalked forward behind the screen that hid the main controls. Giles himself turned back to his own console and reached in to take control of the rods.

On his screen, which had come alive again the moment he had touched the rods, he could now see a section of the opened outer door of the airlock and the spacesuited figure

of the Engineer emerging slowly on the outer hull. There
was a grating sound beyond the wall Giles faced as the
magnetic-soled boots of the Engineer took hold on the
hull and alternately slid forward one by one, with each
step the alien made. The Engineer headed toward the stern
of the vessel, his full figure now showing in Giles' screen
with the lines of the umbilicals trailing behind him. A moment later there was another grating, and the figure of the
Engineer, which had been diminishing in size, began to
swell again as whatever vehicle supported the waldoes
and camera eye of Giles' control console began also to
slide over the hull in pursuit.

This movement across the hull surface was plainly being
controlled by the Captain. Giles found he had nothing to
do, and simply stood, waiting. His vehicle eventually
caught up and stopped just behind the Engineer, who was
now at the very stern of the vessel and slowly unhousing
the shielding over the propulsion motors there.

Tentatively, Giles advanced one of his mechanical hands
to help the spacesuited figure.

"Stop!"

It was the voice of the Captain, speaking in Albenareth
from a grille in the console before Giles.

"Do nothing until I order it, Adelman," the Captain's
voice went on. *"You are unfamiliar with our mechanical
and more likely to do damage to the motors than help. I
repeat, do nothing until I order you to."*

"Very well," answered Giles.

He released his grip on the rods, but continued to hold
them lightly and stood watching what went on in the
screen. The Engineer, clearly, needed to tear down a good
part of one of the motors in order to reach what he had
to repair. It was a slow business—not merely because of
the amount of work involved but because every movement
the Engineer made was made under the clumsiness im-
posed by his spacesuit and the lack of gravity.

"Sir," said Biset's voice at Giles' elbow, in Esperanto.

He had dropped his earlier conversation with her from his
mind entirely. It came flooding back to him now, and he
turned to look at her without taking his hands off the rods.

"Oh, yes," he answered in the same language. *"You
were going to tell me how you came to know Esperanto."*

"No, sir," she said. *"I was going to warn you that on
board here—"*

"First things first," he interrupted her, quietly but with an edge to his voice that should check any impulse on her part to argue the point. *"First, I want to hear how you can speak this language—and, more important, how you happened to guess I could, too."*

"As for the language," she answered, *"I was given a special course in it. As for knowing you, yourself, could speak it, Honor, sir, I was informed of that. Both things were done so that I could communicate with you privately as I'm now doing. Now, if you will allow me to tell you—"*

"Oh yes, about the Black Thursday matter." He had had a few seconds now to gather his wits since this second appearance of hers, and it occurred to him that the best defense here might be to meet her halfway—or better. *"Something about one of their group being aboard, here."*

Her eyes were small and sharp.

"You know about the Black Thursday revolutionaries, then?" she asked.

"I've heard a good deal about them in the past," he said lightly. *"I was something of a revolutionary myself in my younger days when I was still putting over fifty percent of my time in study."*

"Yes," she said. *"We're aware you were a friend of Paul Oca's, and a member of his so-called Philosophical Group. But you parted with that group some years since, didn't you?"*

He looked at her grimly.

"Biset," he said—and now his tone was wholly that of an Adelman speaking to an arbite—*"I think you're forgetting your manners."*

But she did not cower. She stiffened.

"Pardon me, Honor, sir," she said, *"but that is one thing I never do. I told you, I was raised in a good family. Under different conditions I . . . might even have been part of that family."*

So that explained it—as it could as well have explained Mara's differentness and signs of good breeding. Giles took a more compassionate look at the tight face opposite. If life was not easy on an arbite brought up as the pet of some Adelborn, it was a great deal less easy on a half-caste, some arbite born on the wrong side of an Adelborn blanket. There was no place for anyone like that among the Adelborn themselves, and rumor had it that the ordinary arbites hated and despised anyone of their own who carried Adelborn blood in her—or him.

"Forgive me, Biset," he said, in a gentler tone, *"but your questioning was getting a little personal, you know."*

"It's not for myself I question or speak," she said, and her pale eyes flashed momentarily like winter ice in a glimpse of sunlight from a cloud-thick sky. *"I am the voice of the Police."*

He chilled a little, inside—but he had the signs of his reaction under calm face.

"I see," he said, quietly. *"Of course, that makes a difference. But these are pretty strange statements you're making. What would a member of an arbite revolutionary group be doing, going as an indent to Belben? Certainly, someone like that would want to stay on Earth, where they could be useful to whatever plans the organization has."*

"We don't know the answer to that, yet," said Biset. *"But it's a fact that many of the Colony Worlds are more lax than they should be in reporting the presence of criminals from Earth back to the World Police. Witness the fact that your former friend Paul Oca is thought to have left Earth for one of those colony installations."*

So, thought Giles, the World Police had joined the Oca Front in their conclusion about Paul's whereabouts. That meant he must find Paul before the Police did, if there was to be any hope of a successful assassination. The Police were limited by law to attempts at rehabilitation that in no way forced or damaged a criminal's personality. Their methods, of analysis and discussive persuasion, worked well enough on the circumscribed minds of arbites. They would never dent the educated intellect and will of an Adelborn like Paul; and Paul, under Police guard, would continue to survive as a symbol for the arbite revolutionaries, who could go on recruiting in his name.

"Is he?" Giles said, now. *"I wonder how he got there."*

"He had help—from the Black Thursday organization, we believe," Biset answered. *"In fact, whoever it is aboard who belongs to that organization may be a courier to him."*

"Oh?" said Giles.

A sudden, sharp interest kindled in him. If this woman was right and he could find out who the Black Thursday courier was before she did, the courier might be able to lead him directly to Paul. Of course that would mean protecting the Black Thursday member long enough to let him or her make contact—and that in turn might make necessary the killing of Biset. The deep training of a lifetime rose in him against the thought. It was bad enough to have to kill an equally competent member of his own class, like Paul. To murder a helpless arbite, one of the class he and his family had dedicated their generations to guiding toward the day when no one need be bound to a lifetime on the wheel of duty any longer, that was—

He blocked further thought on that topic, deliberately. What needed to be done would have to be done. There was no turning aside from necessity. If he must kill an arbite to reach Paul, then he must kill an arbite . . . that was all there was to it.

"Honor, sir," the voice of Biset jarred on his ear, *"are you listening to me?"*

"What? Oh, forgive me," said Giles. *"I have to keep part of my attention on the screen, here."* He nodded at the screen of his instrument console, which showed the Engineer still at work on the motors.

"Of course. I'd forgotten. Forgive me instead, sir," she said. *"But what I have to tell you is important. I was saying that while I've got no actual proof yet who the Black Thursday member is, I am already fairly certain in my own mind. I'm sure it's the girl called Mara."*

"Mara!" Her name came from Giles' lips a little more forcefully than he liked.

"Yes, sir," Biset was saying, *"and that's why I'm speaking to you about it now. I need definite proof, or the girl's admission to some third-party witness, before I can do more than hold her for temporary questioning once we reach Belben; and you'd be surprised how some of these hard-core arbite revolutionaries can resist and avoid making an arrestible admission during the period of temporary questioning the law allows us."*

"Of course," murmured Giles, his mind spinning with this information. *"I'll help in any way I can."*

"The Adelman needn't involve himself unduly . . ." Biset was saying, but Giles hardly heard her. Much to his own surprise, a section of his mind was rejecting vigorously the notion that Mara could be in any way connected with the Black Thursday group. That organization's name dated back to a wild attempt by a group of obviously self-deluded arbites to force their way into a session of the Adelborn

Council—the decision-making body for all Earth. The arbites had been carrying banners and placards calling on the Council to shorten the term of the lifetime work contracts presently required for lower-class education.

Naturally, the protesters had been unarmed. . . . All, that was, but one of them. One young man had a stolen Police shortgun from the depot where he was on contract as a warehouseman. He was foolish enough to produce this weapon, which he probably did not even know how to fire, and wave it around. Naturally, the Council guards themselves opened fire, and the protesters were cut into smoking ruins.

The day had been a Thursday, and this newer, grimmer, underground organization among the arbites had chosen to name itself the Black Thursday. Its members were a far cry from simple neurotic placard-carriers. The rumor was that they boasted of the weapons each one carried; and the few suspected individuals the Police had been able to round up had reportedly carried poison capsules they had been able to swallow as soon as they had been arrested and before they could be interviewed and questioned.

It was an ugly sort of fanaticism, Giles thought, that would lead a man or woman—even an arbite man or woman—to choose death rather than the possibility of being argued out of obsession with that fanaticism, back into rationality and a useful life. Try as he might, he could not see Mara as that type of irrational. He remembered her smile as she had commented that picking *ib* fruit was not the most demanding job in existence. The kind of person who could be a Black Thursday member with a poison capsule hidden about him could not be the sort of person to joke and smile like that, certainly. No, it was unthinkable. . . .

He roused himself from his thoughts.

"Sorry," he said to Biset. *"I got occupied for a moment with what the Engineer's doing there. Would you tell me again?"*

"I was saying, Honor, sir," Biset repeated, *"there's no need for you to put yourself to the trouble of any unusual effort, or any action unbecoming an Adelborn. The girl is young and you are, after all, of the opposite sex and of the higher classes. It's not unknown that an Adelman . . ."*

Uncharacteristically, for once, Biset's voice wavered. She caught herself up sharply and went on.

"It's not unknown that an Adelman should find himself attracted—temporarily, of course—to an arbite. And of course these Black Thursday people like to think they're as good as any Adelborn. I'm sure if your Honor will simply avoid rejecting her when she finally gets to the point of making advances to you, you'll soon have her talking quite freely to you. The minute she says anything compromising, you need only tell me. I'll take charge from that point on."

"You're that sure, are you," demanded Giles, "that she'll make advances, as you put it, to me?"

"I'm positive of it," said Biset, crisply. "A man—pardon me, sir—an Adelborn like you doesn't know these arbites the way I do. They'd all sell their soul to be one of the upper classes."

Giles looked at her tight-held lips. She was probably right, he told himself, glumly, but somehow it was sickening to hear her put it in words like that. Well, duty was duty, and in this case it was as much in the interest of the Oca Front as of the Police to see the Black Thursday arbites captured, or put out of business. But who could have thought that pretty, bright-looking little Mara—

A new thought exploded suddenly on the battleground of his mind. He looked sharply at Biset.

"Just a second," he said. *"We're forgetting something. You say you're a member of the Police, but I've only got your word for that, or for any of this you've been telling me. For all I know you could be a Black Thursday member yourself, and Mara could belong to the Police."*

"Of course, sir. Quite right," she answered.

Her fingers went to the tab at the top of the vertical seal line of her coveralls, hesitated a second, then grasped the tab and pulled it down no more than a couple of inches. The coverall collar gaped open, revealing the thin, corded column of her neck, shadowed within. Against the dimness of that shadow, something tiny burned and glowed like a speck of living green fire.

Giles frankly stared. He had heard of the Police identispores, but had never seen one before in his life. What he was looking at, he knew, was a miniature bubble of crystalline transparency, in the heart of which was buried a special spore, the cultivation of which was one of the most jealously guarded secrets of the Police and the Council. The bubble would be glued with a physiological glue to the flesh of Biset's neck, and from the bubble itself a nearly invisible hair of a tube would be reaching down into a nearby blood vessel. Up that tube, as up a capillary, some of Biset's blood would reach and nourish the spore, which —as long as it was alive—would glow with its own, unique color, unlike the color of any of its sister spores.

Removed from its connection with Biset's bloodstream, that spore would die and its individual light would go out. Even if placed immediately in contact with the bloodstream of any other person, it would die. It had been cultured on Biset's individual body chemistry, and any other body chemistry was poison to it.

"My ident card," Biset was saying.

Giles looked down and saw her holding a small white card, also enclosed in a few millimeters of crystalline transparency—a material that made tampering with it almost an impossibility. A perfectly ordinary arbite identification card, except that one corner of it was colored green. Giles took the card from her hand and held it up so that the colored corner was only a fraction of an inch from the minuscule living jewel at her throat. The colors matched.

"Yes," he said, letting his breath out in something that almost became a sigh. *"Thank you. I believe you now."*

He handed back the card. She took it with one hand, resealed the collar of her coveralls with the other.

"I can count on your help then, Honor, sir?"

"Yes, he said, heavily, *"you can count on it. Wait—"* The sudden sharp note in his voice arrested her as she started to turn away.

"The Police serve the Council and the Council represent the Adelborn. I am the only Adelborn here. You'll do what I say—and I say you'll take no steps to arrest or question anyone on this ship without coming and getting my permission first. You'll do nothing whatsoever in the line of Police duty without checking with me first. Is that understood?"

Her face was unreadable. She hesitated for just a second, and in that second, the Captain's voice spoke.

"Now!" it exploded, in Albenareth, suddenly from the grille of the console before Giles. Giles jerked into full alertness. He had let his thoughts run away from him, while his attention was lulled by his own lack of understanding of the purpose behind most of the actions of the Engineer shown on the screen. Now he woke suddenly to the fact that what he had taken for a continuing effort

of work on the part of the spacesuited figure had become a sort of aimless pawing at the cover of the remaining motor, like the fumblings of a drunk man.

"Adelman!" said the Captain's voice. *"Do you hear me? Now you must act. Use your mechanical to take hold of the Engineer. Gently, now—about the body . . . gently . . ."*

Tensely, Giles maneuvered the rods and their finger studs. The alien waldoes were like the equivalent machine of human design in that they were far more powerful than the flesh-and-blood hands directing them; and Giles concentrated on using them as lightly as possible to take hold of the Engineer around what in human terms would have been his waist.

He was too gentle. He got a six-finger grip on the Engineer and then lost it. The spacesuited body bobbled away, floating above the hull of the lifeship, tethered only by its umbilical connections. Giles made a grab for it—but instinctively used two mechanical fingers in the human manner instead of the Albenarethian three, and the Engineer floated free again.

The voice of the Captain shouted something from the grille in front of Giles, but Giles was concentrating too hard on his job at hand to listen or translate what was said. He tried once more, delicately, with all three fingers on each metal arm; and this time he caught the Engineer firmly.

The grating sound rumbled through the hull of the lifeship. In Giles' screen the images of the motors began to shrink as the Captain activated the vehicle carrying Giles' mechanical device and the Engineer back toward the airlock.

"Stand by, Adelman!" said the Captain's voice from the grille—and this time Giles heard and understood him. *"Now comes the difficult part. You will have to lift him around the corner into the airlock, and place him so that he does not float out when I close the outer lock door."*

Giles grunted. No doubt it would be a maneuver that any trained Albenareth could accomplish without thinking. But for an untrained human like himself, it was as delicate as balancing a plate on edge and then letting go of it to reach for another plate to balance on top of the first. He must release the Engineer with both waldoes, hoping that the alien would hold his position on the lip of the airlock while Giles got a new grip from another angle that would allow him to move the Engineer all the way inside the lock. If he fumbled, the Engineer would drift out of his present position, and the two-move series would have to begin all over again. And the Engineer—if he was not already dead —was coming closer to death by the minute.

A little, distant section of Giles' mind took this moment to laugh at him. Here he was straining every effort to save the life of a being to whom death was the greatest of rewards, and the culmination of all other rewards. But, strangely, knowing that the Albenareth thought so made no difference to Giles' body and mind in this moment. He was not Albenareth; he was human. And the pattern of humans was to fight death in themselves or in anyone for whom they felt love or responsibility, down to the last moment of hope, and the last line of defense.

Delicately, Giles freed his six mechanical fingers from their grasp on the middle part of the spacesuited figure. Quickly, he rotated both the finger-support rods, to change the whole angle of their attack on the body they were trying to lift. Then he moved them in for another six-finger grip on the Engineer.

The Engineer had already begun to float away from contact with the lifeship; but Giles, operating above himself under the adrenaline of the moment, made a fair recatch of the other's figure with all six fingers of the two mechanical hands. For a second he merely held position, waiting for the wave of relief to pass, then slowly he began to swing the Engineer down into the airlock itself.

The move inside went smoothly, but the bight of the umbilicals still floated out into space, through the open outer door. They would keep the outer door from sealing properly, unless they were also brought full into the lock.

Giles risked a great deal. He had been so aware of his inability to use the two hands of the waldoes separately that he had not even practiced doing so. But now, with the Engineer safely within the lock, he could not risk letting the spacesuited alien float out again. Delicately, he concentrated on holding the Engineer down upon the airlock floor with one mechanical hand, while with the other he reached for the umbilicals.

For a moment he felt the division of attention and frustration that anyone feels who is trying for the first time the old trick of patting his head with one hand while rubbing his stomach in a circular motion with the other. Then his groping mechanical fingers hooked the floating umbilicals and drew them back into the airlock.

They were barely inside the lock when the outer door began to close. Clearly the Captain had been watching and had no intention of letting a second be lost. When the outer lock door was swung to sufficiently so that neither Engineer nor umbilicals could escape to block its closing, Giles unwrapped his aching hands from around the two rods, turned about, and slumped against the inner hull of the lifeship, panting. His upper suit was soaked with sweat and clung to him.

The Captain had been right. What Giles had just done had been no job for an arbite. It had required not only a healthy body in good nervous and physical condition, but someone with enough personal self-confidence to gamble on the abilities of that body. . . . Giles woke suddenly to the fact that he had an audience. All the arbites on the ship, it seemed, with Mara and Biset in their front rank, were clustered just beyond the gap in the first screen, silently watching him.

He opened his mouth to order them back, but the voice of the Captain, buzzing loudly on the human words, beat him to it.

"Back! Out! Adelman, tell your people to get out of our way—and help me after I open the lock!"

"You heard him!" panted Giles. "Get back. Sit down on your cots. Stay out of the way. We'll be coming through with the Engineer in a minute and I want the way open!"

They melted away before him. He turned to join the Captain, but the Albenareth motioned him back.

"Stop!" said the alien, in her own language. *"Touch him and you'll injure yourself!"*

The Captain was right, Giles saw, as the inner airlock door slowly swung wide to reveal the Engineer. His spacesuit was covered with frost, as the whole inner part of the lock had been when they had first opened it, and was again now. The Captain stepped forward into the lock, extending hands around which she had once more wrapped plastic sheeting for protection. Awkwardly, but swiftly, she disconnected the umbilicals and lifted the motionless figure of the Engineer through the inner lock door into the body of the lifeship.

"Go ahead of me," she said to Giles. *"Make sure the way is clear to the rear area of the ship. By the time we*

*get back there, his suit will be warm enough for you to
touch safely."*

"*I understand,*" said Giles.

He walked swiftly in front of the two aliens into the
back area of the lifeship, and the Captain, following him,
brought the figure of the Engineer to a cot that had be-
longed to Di, and laid it down there, clipping the tool
straps from the belt of the spacesuit to the frame of the
cot to hold it in place.

"*Now . . .*" said the Captain.

She unwrapped the plastic from her hands, and gently
setting the powerful three fingers of each hand around the
curve of the helmet, she turned it carefully until its seal
disengaged. There was a little inward-sucking sound of air,
and then the still-frosted helmet came loose in the Captain's hands. She and Giles stood looking down at last on
the face of the Engineer.

To Giles, there was little to be read from what he saw.
The Engineer's eyes were closed, and his dark skin had an
ashy color, as though it had been lightly dusted with gray
powder. It was impossible for human eyes to tell whether
he breathed or not.

"*How is he?*" Giles asked.

"*Good. Some life remains,*" answered the Captain shortly, almost absently, her hands flying about the spacesuit to
undo its lockings and seals. "*Adelman, behind you on the
other cot you will find certain tools—among them a joined
pair of cutters. Use them to remove the ties from the
Engineer's limbs. Do not try to unfasten the clamps. Cut.
Do you understand?*"

"*I understand,*" said Giles.

He turned about and found the cutters of which the Captain had been talking.

In the process of cutting the ties, he saw at close hand
how the ancient spacesuit had, indeed, failed. Around the
body section there had evidently been no leaks. But at
more than one place on each arm or leg where flexing had
occurred, there had been leaks. In each case the ties had
clamped down; and now in the section that had lost air
pressure, the limb of the Engineer showed swollen and
ugly. In cutting the ties, Giles inadvertently touched several
of these swollen sections and they gave slightly, bulging
to his fingertips, like worn inner tubes filled to bursting
with liquid.

The Captain had the upper part of the Engineer stripped of the spacesuit by the time Giles had finished cutting the last of the ties around the engineer's ankles. A moment later and the spacesuit was pulled free of the motionless alien, leaving him lying there in only the shipboard harness both Albenareth were accustomed to wear.

The Engineer's eyes were still closed. He had shown no sign of understanding that they had him back in the lifeship and were working on him. He did not move, but once or twice he had made a faint hissing noise deep in his throat.

"How is he? Will he die?" Giles asked.

"He is dying," said the Captain. She whirled on Giles. *"Go now. Keep your humans out of this back area. I do not want them here. I do not want them looking in here. Is that clear? The last moments of an Albenareth are not a spectacle for aliens."*

"I will stay away and keep all the others away—of course," said Giles. He turned and went out through the gap in the closer screen, into the section where the arbites still waited. Behind him there was a sudden screeching of torn metal. He turned to see the cot which had been Frenco's literally ripped from its supports, being thrust upright into the gap in the back screen to make a barrier there.

The cot did not really fill the gap. There was room on the hull side of the opening for a human to slip through, if he or she wanted to. But it blocked a view of the two aliens from the middle section of the lifeship, and it was a stark symbol of the Captain's demand for privacy.

"I think you all understand what that means," Giles said to the arbites. He was surprised to hear his own tongue thick from exhaustion. He gestured toward the cot blocking the entrance to the rear section of the lifeship. "The Captain has said none of us are to go back there, or look in there. I'll add my own personal order to that. I don't want any of you going close to that opening or sneaking a look—"

He broke off suddenly. For the first time since they had come aboard the lifeship, the blue-white lights overhead that were never turned off and that nourished the growth of the *ib* vine had dimmed. They shone now with only a faint reddishness of illumination; and the abrupt decrease

of light after all these hours left the humans nearly blind
while they waited for their eyes to adjust.

"I repeat," croaked Giles. "Stay away from that rear
section. There's nothing back there you're likely to need."
He nodded meaningfully at the lifeship's primitive sanitary
facilities, which were enclosed by the screens of the middle
section. "Stay here and stay quiet until further order. Not
only will you have me to deal with if you don't, but the
Captain will probably take his own measures—and I can't
promise to protect any one of you, in that case."

He turned, feeling his blind way with both hands, and
stumbled through the gap in the front screen to fumble
for and locate his cot. His hands closed on the edge of it,
he sat down on it, and lay back. Sleep swallowed him at a
gulp. . . .

He was on his feet and moving again before he was
truly awake. The air was being shivered by screams from
some human throat. The overhead lights in the lifeship
were back to a brilliant blue-white. In a staggering plunge
he went toward the noise—through the gap in the nearer
screen and through the knot of arbites who were beginning
to cluster about the cot-blocked gap in the farther screen.
He went past the cot itself, knocking it aside as he burst
into the rear section of the ship. Just as he did so the
screams were stopped as abruptly as if a hand had been
jammed over the mouth of the screamer.

He found himself facing the Captain, who stood holding
Di like a broken doll in long, dark alien hands. The girl
draped limply, eyes closed, in the grasp of the alien. Of
the Engineer there was no sign; but the Captain, the floor
covering, and the one cot that remained were liberally
spotted with dark alien blood.

"*Take her,*" said the Captain, making one step forward
and putting the unconscious form of the girl into Giles'
arms. "*She came back here where she was told not to; but
she is not harmed.*"

Giles accepted the dead weight of Di. He stood holding
her and still staring at the Captain.

"*Where is the Engineer?*" Giles said thickly in Albenareth.

"*He has passed through the further Portal in all honors,*"
said the Captain. She switched abruptly to Basic. "So
much for he that was he. His husk"—the Captain turned

and nodded toward the converter—"is of use and has been put to use."

There was a sickened moan from the arbite group in the screen opening. Giles stared at the converter. The main door on top of it was still propped open slightly. That door was fully large enough to allow insertion of the Engineer's body. There would have been no need to dismember the corpse. Giles looked about and saw the pile of instruments he had seen earlier. None of them was marked with the dark blood so omnipresent otherwise.

"Whose blood is that?" he asked in Albenareth.

"Human," said the Captain, in the same language, *"I am weary of the questions of you and your race!"*

She strode past Giles abruptly, almost knocking him over. The arbites scattered before the tall figure, then flowed back into the rear section to stare at the blood, the converter, and the figure of Di.

Giles himself looked down at Di. On either side of her neck toward the back the dark shadows of bruises were beginning to discolor the skin—two bruises on one side of the neck and one on the other, as might have been made by a very powerful, three-fingered hand.

"What happened?" It was Mara, facing him, reaching down to lift the unconscious girl's head. "Frenco said she had nightmares. She must have woken up from one, forgotten where she was, and started back to her cot, here. But what made her scream like that? What did she see?"

"God knows," said Giles, grimly. He looked down at the closed eyes in the still face. "And if those screams are any indication, I doubt she'll want to remember what it was when she does wake up. We may never know."

Second day—16:15 hours

Giles had been right in his unprofessional guess. When Di came to, after she had been carried to a cot in the middle section, she did not remember. She seemed confused and uncertain, like someone who has just recovered from the effects of a heavy drug. She cried and clung to Mara or Biset, whoever was closest. She threatened to become hysterical if any of the men came near her— including Frenco, whom she did not seem to recognize at all.

In the end, the two other women took turns sitting with her, and bit by bit she dropped into short periods of uneasy sleep, from which she was as likely to wake screaming as not. But, gradually, the violence of her nightmares seemed to diminish, and she began to sleep for longer and more normal periods. Still, she did not remember anything of what she had seen in the stern area of the lifeship. Her last memory was of the Engineer being brought back through the airlock.

Frenco, meanwhile, in the space of less than twenty-four hours, went from a round-faced boy to a pale, sharp-featured man on the edge of violence. He could not believe that Di did not want him near her and was ready to fight his way to her. In the end, Giles had to appoint Hem to guard the girl against Frenco's approaches.

Meanwhile, the rest of the humans were close to a condition of total anarchy. With the exception of Hem, who was apparently undisturbed by the disposition of the Engineer's body, and Giles, who forced himself to eat, none of the others would touch the pulp of the fruit from the *ib* vine. Indeed, with the exception of Hem and Giles, the humans held off drinking the *ib* juice until thirst literally drove them to it. But eat they would not. Finally, Giles called them all together in the center section between the screens.

"Now listen to me," he said. "Try to understand. We're out here alone in space, surrounded by light-years of emptiness, and this lifeship is the only thing we have to give us a chance of ever making it to planetfall again. If we ever get out of this alive, what we'll have to thank will be the lifeship and the Captain—yes, the Engineer, too. Don't look away from me when I say that. Make an effort to think outside all the things you grew up with and learned and took for granted. What we have here—this closed cycle with the converter—is exactly the same kind of closed cycle we had back on Earth, only simplified. . . . Look at me when I talk to you!"

Pale faces that had been averted turned back to him. That much he could make them do—obey the physical command. Whether he could actually get them to think in terms of this new and alien environment was something else again. Well, at least he could try.

"I want you to look at matters squarely, with your feelings set aside," he went on. "The drive motors needed to be worked on. That is a *fact*. The Engineer had to go outside and work on them, at the cost of his life, which was a price he expected to pay. Another *fact*. It did cost him his life; and the Captain, rather than letting go to waste nutrients which would help keep us alive—us humans, remember, not just some equivalent number of individuals of his own race—put the Engineer's body in the recycling tank to feed the *ib* vine. *Fact*. There they are—facts. Not matters of opinion which you can choose to react to or not to react to—but facts. Because if you don't accept them as the facts they are, the final fact of all will get you—if you don't eat, you'll die."

"Kept him alive, too . . ." muttered a male voice.

"Who's that? Esteven?" Giles stared at the entertaincom. Unlike the others, Esteven was not particularly pale. If anything, he was a little flushed and there was a glazed, defiant look to his eyes. "What do you mean—kept who alive, too?"

"I mean him—the Captain!" said Esteven, more loudly. "He lives off the *ib* vine, too—and the Engineer. I say he was keeping himself alive by putting the Engineer in there —Honor, sir!"

The last two words were uttered almost impudently. But Giles paid little attention. He was busy adjusting his own mind. He had forgotten that the arbites believed the Albenareth Captain to be a male. For a moment he toyed with the idea of telling them the truth about the alien commander's sex, then rejected it. The less confusion and surprise aboard from now on, the better.

"The Albenareth don't fight the prospect of death the way we do, Esteven," Giles said, evenly. "You know that. What makes the Captain run is a sense of duty, not personal worries."

"Pardon me, Honor, sir," said Esteven. The ordinarily quiet and withdrawn man was acting far out of his usual character at the moment. He was almost belligerent. "But are you sure about that?"

It was time to sit on him, thought Giles.

"When I tell you anything, Esteven," he said, harshly and finally, "you can take it for granted that I'm sure about it, or I wouldn't say it. Now, unless you've got something more useful to say, I want you to sit there and be quiet. Do you understand?"

"Yes, Honor, sir . . ." All at once the belligerence went out of the arbite. He shrank back into his usual silence and inconspicuousness.

"All right," said Giles, turning to the others. "I'm not going to order you to eat. I'm going to appeal to you to try to eat; and until you do, all of you are going to be required to sit here, twice a ship-day, and watch while Hem and I eat. And that first meal is going to be right now. . . . Hem?"

The big laboring arbite got up, stepped into the rear section, and returned with two bowls of the *ib* pulp. He handed one to Giles and sat down on a cot with the other.

Giles ate stolidly, hiding his own feelings about the Engineer and the vine pulp under the mask of indifference he had learned during that first year after being sent away to boarding school. Hem was truly indifferent. The watching arbites sat silently, bearing up very well under the scene they were witnessing—until the very end, when Hem thoughtlessly began to lick the stray pulp from his fingers and first Di, then Groce and Frenco, were abruptly sick, crowding into the sanitary cubicle with little energy left over to be considerate of one another.

Much of the same scene was repeated six hours later, and again for three more times before Biset and Mara, at once, sat down with bowls holding hardly more than a tablespoonful apiece of the *ib* pulp and choked it down. Two mealtimes later and they were all eating, including Di.

Meanwhile, Di and Frenco had moved back into the spurious privacy of the rear section of the lifeship. Another cot had been pulled up from the floor to take the place of the one the Captain had torn from its fastening to bar the entrance in the screen. The rest were all in the center section with the exception of Hem, who had moved to a cot up in the front section where Giles had been by himself until the Engineer's death.

It was a curiously forward thing for the low-graded bumper to do on his own initiative, but Giles thought it best not to question the man about it. Most arbites of Hem's type, questioned about anything, became over-whelmed with embarrassment and tongue-tied with the fear of not giving the proper answers. Meanwhile, things were going as smoothly as could be expected, now that all the humans were finally adjusted to the lifeship's environ-ment and eating correctly once more. Giles turned over the situation in his own mind. It was one in which ordi-narily he would offer the arbites some kind of reward to reinforce the positive effect of their good behavior. But here on the lifeship, rewards were not easily available.

He hit finally on a farfetched possibility. He must talk to the Captain anyway, and that conversation would pro-vide an opportunity for the asking of a special considera-tion. He waited until several ship-days after the death of the Engineer before approaching the other Albenareth.

Choosing a time when the arbites were all in the middle or stern section of the craft, Giles went up to the partition within which the Captain had been keeping herself iso-lated almost continuously since the Engineer's death. Standing outside the screen that hid the alien commander, Giles spoke in Albenareth.

"Captain, I'd like to talk to you." There was a moment's pause, then the sound of the alien voice answered.

"Come."

Giles walked around the edge of the screen and turned

to face the Captain, who was sitting before one of the control consoles. Without getting up, she swiveled her command seat to face him.

"Captain," said Giles, *"perhaps you can tell me now how long it will be before we make planetfall in this lifeship."*

"We will reach Belben in a little less than a hundred and eight ship-days."

"I see," said Giles. *"That is a long time."*

"It is the time required," said the Captain. There was no difference that Giles' human ear could find in the Albenareth's tones, and no difference that he could see in the way she sat or spoke. But still, something about her conveyed an impression of remoteness, as if she had somehow put a new distance, not only between her and himself, but between her and the lifeship with everyone else aboard it.

"I take it there is no better destination?" asked Giles.

"There is no other destination."

"If the Captain will bear with me," said Giles. He had a feeling as if he was walking through some strange field sowed with booby traps and mines that he could not imagine, much less see. What he had to say skirted the dangerous perimeter of alien emotions, alien honor. *"There is a human mining colony together with an Albenareth spaceship station, on a world called 20B-40, according to our charts. Out of interest, I studied those charts before leaving on this voyage. I have no skill at navigation, of course, beyond piloting my own small craft within my own Solar System; but unless I am mistaken, at this moment 20B-40 would be only perhaps half the distance from us that Belben is."*

"Perhaps," said the Captain. *"However, Belben is our destination."*

"Why, when 20B-40 is closer?"

"Belben was our original destination. My ship has been lost, but some honor may be saved if what is left of her passengers are delivered as promised."

"What honor will there be in delivering them, if they are not then living?" Giles asked. *"A hundred and eight days is a long time for these people of mine to survive under these conditions."*

"Survive?" said the Captain. *"Oh yes, I had forgotten how you humans, having no knowledge of the Way and its Portals, shrink and scurry from the thought of Passing.*

*But that is your affair. My duty was only that of delivery—
alive or dead are all one to me."*

"They are not to me," said Giles. "I have a responsibility
to keep these of my own race alive. I ask you to pilot us
instead to 20B-40."

"No," said the Captain. She closed her eyes as if she
was very tired. "I can afford no more departures from the
Way."

"Captain," said Giles, slowly. "I am of the house and
sept of Steel, and Steel has great wealth, part of which I
command personally. If you will turn aside to 20B-40 I
will give you my promise—and the promise of an Adelborn is a contract signed—to either pay you whatever is
necessary to build you another ship just like the one you
lost, or pay to actually have it built by your own people
first, and then present it to you. You will have lost nothing,
then."

The Captain opened her eyes and looked at him for a
second.

"But I will have lost," she said. "You are an alien and
do not understand. All my crew and officers, now that the
Engineer has Passed, won death in the destruction of my
ship. To have the ship alone replaced is a hollow thing. It
would pleasure me only; but it would be an insult to the
honors of my crew and officers who have now gone through
the further Portal, if I were to accept something they
could not share and which did them no honor."

She stopped speaking. Giles stood without moving, staring down at her, momentarily without recourse. His offer
to her had been the equivalent of holding out a fortune
to a pauper. In all his plans for this moment it had never
occurred to him that this last and greatest possible price
would be refused.

"You are right, Captain," he said, slowly. "I do not
understand. But I would like to. Perhaps if I understood,
there might be some way we could come to other under-
standings. Can you not explain matters to me so I will
comprehend?"

"No," said the Captain. "There is no responsibility upon
me to make you understand, and none upon you to understand."

"I fail to agree with you," said Giles. "For a long time
now I have believed that the Albenareth and humanity
are bound together in more ways than just those of trade

and shipping. There is not only a duty but a need on us to understand each other, as individuals and as members of our respective races."

"Your opinion is of no consequence," said the Captain. "What you believe is not even possible. You are not of the Albenareth, which is to say you are not of The People. Therefore you would never be able to understand the ways of The People, no matter what efforts I or any other should make to bring you to understanding."

"I think," said Giles, "that what you have just said is not true. I think it is an opinion of yours, only, and that it is that opinion which is wrong, not my own. I ask only that you try."

"No," said the Captain. "To try any such thing would take strength. My strength is now limited. I will not waste it on useless effort."

"It is not useless," said Giles. "It is vital to you and your honor. It is vital to me and my honor. It is vital to the lives of my arbites. It is vital to your race and mine, who may both go down into extinction unless some closer understanding can be found."

The Captain closed her eyes again.

"This matter is no longer discussible," she said. "On what other subjects did you wish to speak to me?"

Giles opened his mouth, then closed it again.

"There is more ib vine and fruit of the vine than is needed for as small a party, such as we are presently in this lifeship," he said. "At the time of the Engineer's passing, the lights were turned down to a less bright mode. It would be a great help to my people in enduring this voyage if the lights could be turned down at regular intervals for short periods. Surely the ib vine can supply us with sufficient nourishment in spite of short periods of lessened illumination."

"The light must remain constant," said the Captain, without opening her eyes. "All things must remain as they are until we reach our appointed destination. Now, Adelman, I am weary of talking and wish privacy."

"Very well," said Giles. "I will talk no more with you—now."

He turned and went back to his cot. He sat down on it, his mind whirling. There had to be a way to make the Captain change their destination to the mining colony on the nearer world. He became aware suddenly that Hem was seated on his own cot, silently watching.

"Don't just sit here!" said Giles, irritated by the big bumper's silent stare. "Do something with yourself. Go back and talk to some of the others. They're never going to include you in things as long as you hide off by yourself this way!"

Without a word, Hem got up and stepped back through the gap in the screen into the middle section of the ship where most of the other arbites were.

"And the rest of you back in there!" added Giles, raising his voice. "Hem's one of you on board here, and I want you to react to him the same way you would to any of the rest of you! Remember that!"

A corner of his mind nibbled at him with small teeth, reminding him that he was taking out his own frustration with the Captain on the arbites, who dared not frustrate him in anything. But he forced himself to ignore the thought. He stretched out on the cot and threw a forearm across his eyes to shut out the never-ending ceiling illumination. Maybe if he slept on the problem he could come up with some idea for changing the Captain's mind.

He woke some time later. There were no arbite voices in conversation sounding beyond the screen next to his cot, but he had the impression that something, some noise, had awakened him. He listened, but all he could hear was the faintest of sounds—almost a sort of struggling-to-breathe sound.

He sat up silently and swung his legs over the end of his cot. From this position he could see through the gap in the near screen to the cots of the middle section. Each one was occupied by a sleeping figure, but it was from none of them that the faint sound was coming—nor was it from beyond the further screen, where Di and Frenco would be.

Puzzled, Giles sat listening. Slowly, his hearing began to get a directional fix on the sound. It came from close by. In fact, it came from the cot across the center aisle from him, the only cot besides his own pulled into up position in the front part of the lifeship.

Hem was sleeping there, lying on his side with his clenched fists up in front of his face, his heavy body curled up on the long but narrow cot. Or was the bumper actually asleep? Silently, Giles got to his feet and stepped over to stand by the head of Hem's cot.

The big arbite was crying—in all but perfect silence. His two heavy fists were hiding his face and somehow he had managed to pull loose enough of the fabric covering his cot to stuff into his mouth and muffle the sounds he was making. He lay there on his side, his mouth hidden by the fists and the fabric, and the tears running down from his tightly shut eyes.

Giles frowned.

"Hem," he said softly.

The bumper did not respond.

"Hem!" Giles said again, no more loudly, but with more tension in his voice. Hem's eyes flew open and stared up at Giles in what might be either astonishment or panic.

"Hem, what's wrong?" Giles asked.

Hem shook his head, tears rolling down his cheeks.

Giles gazed down at him for a moment, perplexed. Then Giles sat down on the floor beside the cot, so that his lips were close to the arbite's ear and he could talk very quietly indeed.

"All right, Hem," he said, softly. "Now you can tell me what's wrong."

Again, Hem shook his head.

"Yes, you can," Giles went on, keeping his voice gentle but insistent. "Something's bothering you. What is it, now?"

Hem struggled with himself and finally lifted the muffling fabric from his mouth long enough to say one, almost inaudible, word.

"Nothing . . ."

"It can't be 'nothing,' " said Giles. "Look at you. Now tell me what is it that's troubling you? Or who is it? Answer me."

"I'm sick," whispered Hem.

"Sick? How? What kind of sickness?"

But Hem had the fabric back in his mouth and was saying nothing.

"Hem," said Giles, still gently, "when I ask you a question, I want you to answer me. Where do you feel sick—in your stomach?"

Hem shook his head.

"Where? In your arm or leg? In your head?"

Hem shook his head to all these suggestions.

"What kind of sickness is it?" demanded Giles. "Do you hurt someplace?"

Hem shook his head. Then he closed his eyes and nodded. His tears began to flow heavily again.

"Well, where, then?" Giles asked.

Hem shuddered. Still keeping his eyes closed, he took the fabric from his mouth.

"Yes," he whispered.

" 'Yes' . . . what? What hurts? Your head—arms—legs? Where?"

Hem only shook his head silently. Giles checked his temper, which was threatening to rise. It was not Hem's fault he could not express himself. The responsibility to find words for what was wrong with the big bumper lay not with the arbite who had only a limited vocabulary, but the Adelman who *could* express himself.

"Tell me if you can, Hem," said Giles. "Just when did you start to feel bad? Was it just after we got into the lifeship? Or just a few hours ago? Or did you feel bad when you were back on the big spaceship?"

Then, at last, it began to come out, in bits and pieces of disjointed sentences. Hem, it seemed, was the exception to what Mara had claimed for all the arbites. The last thing in the world Hem had wanted was to be indent to one of the outer worlds. The reason for this, Giles became aware, had much to do with the status and purpose of Hem's own life back on Earth, a status and purpose Giles had known about all his life but had never appreciated until this moment.

The heavy-duty arbites, those males specially bred to the few hard physical tasks that remained, were essentially a culture apart from the rest of the working class. To keep them from becoming discontented with the relatively simple, repetitive tasks they had to do, they were gene-controlled for a low intelligence level and for those factors that would encourage a feeling of docility and dependence upon their superiors. Theoretically, they were as free as the other arbites. Once in a while, one of them succeeded in leaving the work barracks and setting up a permanent family relationship with some normal arbite woman, but this was uncommon.

For all the strength in their oversize bodies, they were timid socially. Most of them lived out their relatively short lives—for some reason they were more than normally vulnerable to diseases, especially pneumonia, and few of

them in the barracks lived beyond their middle thirties—
almost exclusively in the company of their work-mates.

Hem had been like the rest. To him, the barracks had
been the whole world, and his beer-mate, Jase, the closest
thing to any kind of family he knew. Conceived, essentially,
in a test tube, raised in a nursery reserved exclusively for
low-intelligence boys like himself, and graduated to the
work barracks at the early maturity of thirteen years of
age, Hem had been in no way prepared psychologically to
be torn from the only way of life he knew and sent light-
years away with no company but that of the superior
arbites who had little in common with him. Everything
that Hem knew had been taken from him. He would never
again have a barracksful of old friends to return to. He
would never again know the friendly drinking and the
equally friendly brawls of the beer-busts, the jokes, the
tricks, the pleasure of working in company with his mates.
Above all, he would never see Jase again.

It was a little while before Giles began to put together
the incoherent and broken whispers of the big man. What
he heard opened his eyes to the fallacy of a great many
comforting beliefs he, like everyone else, had always accepted about this lowest class of arbites, without ever stop-
ping to examine them. Those of Hem's special type were
supposed to be incorrigibly cheerful because of their ignorance, automatically brave because they did not have the
intelligence to know the meaning of fear, and totally un-
self-conscious because their size and strength made them
indifferent to the opinions of the weaker, but more intelligent humans around them.

None of this was true, he now learned. But the discovery
still left him puzzled. Something more than just the difference between his actual nature and the way others thought
of him was chewing at Hem. Giles kept after the arbite
with gentle, but prodding questions and finally, in the same
fragmentary fashion in which Hem had expressed himself
about other things, the deeper problem came out.

The important thing for Hem had been his work-mate
Jase. Whether the relationship Hem was trying to describe
had been a homosexual one or not hardly mattered in the
childlike terms of which Hem thought of such things. The
important point was that nobody had loved Hem—mother,
father, sibling, or girl friend. Only Jase. And Hem had returned that affection. For twelve years of barracks life they

had been beer-mates, which in essence meant they did their after-hours drinking always in each other's company.

Then suddenly Hem was taken away, to be shipped to some strange colony on a different world, where it was doubtful that there would be even one other laboring-class arbite for him to talk to. He could not even write Jase— not because he was illiterate, but because it was too much of a creative demand for someone like himself to make a letter anything but an emotionless vehicle for the simplest sort of factual information.

So, suffering under this loss, with his grief completely unsuspected by everyone around him, including his so-called fellow arbites, Hem had stumbled even deeper into emotional trouble. He had no name for the new pain within him; he could not even consciously connect with its cause—but Giles, eking the information out of him bit by unhappy bit, came to understand what Hem could not admit, even to himself.

Simply, it was that Hem, robbed of Jase, had needed desperately to find someone else to fasten his affections up-on. And unconsciously, he had fastened them finally on Giles. Giles, alone among the aliens and upper-caste arbites that now surrounded Hem, showed some of the size, the strength, the characteristics that Hem associated with his own mates.

And the big arbite's reaction was not so much to wonder at, at that, thought Giles silently. He contrasted his own early days in boarding school with Hem's. He and the bumper had been at opposite ends of the social spectrum; but in both cases the irresistible hand of custom and authority had picked them up, molded them, and deter-mined the life they would lead while they were still too young to know what was being done to them. They were equally damned—no, thought Giles, Hem was the better of the two in one respect. He had been left with the freedom to love—even if it was only one of his mates. Giles had had a close relationship with Paul Oca as perhaps he had never had with any other man, but it could not really be said that they were "mates," even in the ordinary, work meaning of that word in Hem's barracks.

As for girls . . . women, it came to Giles suddenly that he had given nothing worthwhile in any of his brief liaisons, and had been scrupulously careful to take nothing. For the first time it occurred to him that no one had ever loved him, and he also had really never loved anyone. His own parents had been there in the flesh, but removed from him across barriers of age and manners. His brothers and sisters, if he had ever had any, would have been brought up apart from him to become polite strangers. He did not miss this lack of an affection that was one of the necessary ingredients of life itself to Hem; but he was not unaware of its existence. For him, love was duty and duty love. That was as far as his emotions would go—and he could see no hope of there ever being anything more for him.

His thoughts came back to Hem. Unconsciously, Hem had taken hold of one of Giles' hands in his own two big fists and was holding it, weeping over it in the depths of his voiceless unhappiness. Hem, Giles realized, would never be able to understand why he was suffering. The perhaps lucky thing about Hem's affection for Giles was that while the bumper felt it, he was completely incapable of acknowledging it. The very suggestion that he might dream of someone like an Adelman being a "mate" to him in any sense of the word was so far out of context with life as Hem knew it that he was mercifully protected from entertaining it consciously. The only way he could approach such a thought was in the desperate wish to do something for Giles, something large and terrible, up to the giving of his life for the Adelman. He tried to tell Giles so, in fragmentary phrases.

"Good," said Giles. "That's very good, Hem. I appreciate it. Don't worry. If ever I need you, I'll call you—right away."

"You will?" said Hem.

"Of course," said Giles. "Of course. Don't let it worry you, Hem. Everything's going to be all right."

"It is?" Hem relaxed at last. He still cried, but now it was out of relief and gratitude—he could not have said why, any more than he had been able earlier to identify the cause of his unhappiness. He clung to Giles' hand and wept.

Giles sat with him patiently for a little while longer, until the bumper dropped off into sleep. Then gently withdrawing his hand, Giles stood up and stretched stiff muscles. He was cramped from sitting cross-legged on the floor of the lifeship. Stretching, he made a mental note to find out, once they made planetfall, where, if at all, there were other heavy-laboring arbites stationed on the Colony Worlds. It would probably be impossible to get Hem returned to Earth, but it should not be beyond the bounds of impossibility to get his indent changed to someplace where he could be with work-mates of his own stamp, if any such place existed on one of the Colony Worlds.

Meanwhile, Giles lay down again on his own cot and closed his eyes. There must be some means of convincing the Captain to change the lifeship's course to 20B-40. Now that he knew that the World Police also believed Paul was on one of the Colony Worlds, they might have men and women out on those worlds hunting Paul now. Time had become a factor in the assassination. Giles had never anticipated that the alien officer, whoever that might be, in charge of the lifeship, would be this stubborn about maintaining course for the spaceship's original destination.

Why? That was the question. Why was the Captain being so adamant in her refusal to do the sensible thing and head for the nearest safe planetfall? Maybe if he could find out what was motivating her. . . .

7

Two sleep-days later, Giles still was without an answer to his question, a solution to the problem of how to get the lifeship turned toward 20B-40. But he was not destined to be left to puzzle over it in peace. As he sat on his cot with Esteven's recorder, talking the last day's entry into it, there was an explosion of noise from between the screens enclosing the middle section of the ship. Shouts, screams, and the sounds of bodies bumping about.

He shoved the recorder into a pocket and went through the gap in the adjoining screen almost as swiftly as he had gone through it when Di had screamed, at the time of the death of the Engineer. In the middle section, Groce had Esteven pinned up against one wall of the lifeship hull and was doing his best to pound the other arbite into unconsciousness. Groce was obviously a good ten years or more older than Esteven. Also he was the smaller, lighter man and very obviously he had no knowledge of how to fight, beyond a general idea that he should ball his fists and keep swinging them at another person. But his sheer fury was outweighing these small drawbacks. Esteven, caught between two cots and with his back to the metal wall, could not get away from the furious computecom, and it was plain enough that unless he was rescued, Groce was going to succeed eventually in doing him considerable damage.

Giles hurdled a pair of intervening cots and grabbed Groce by the back of the collar and the slack in his coveralls at his waist.

78

"Stop that!" he snapped, pulling the computecom back out of arm's reach of Esteven, who sagged against the wall. "Calm down, Groce. . . . No, no, don't try hitting *me* now. Sit down and be quiet. You, too, Esteven. Sit down on that other cot over there, and tell me what's going on here."

"He—he—" Esteven was almost sobbing. The unnatural flushed look Giles had noticed once before was back on his cheek, and the finger he pointed at Groce trembled. "He's got everything to keep him occupied. He's got a compute. And he's got a book, too. All I wanted was a few pages out of the book so that I could write down some music I've been composing—"

"All!" shouted Groce. The older man's voice scaled upward in outrage. "Just a few pages—that's *all*? A whole handful of pages torn out of my ancestor's book on propositional calculus! I've been working the statements in it, to pass the time. But it's *my* book—and it's priceless! It's over two hundred and twenty-five years old. Do you think I'm going to rip sheets out of a precious family antique like that, just so he can scribble some homemade music notes on it? What's he doing composing music, anyway? Nobody writes any real music nowadays except with a compute-tank—"

"Groce!" said Giles. Groce went silent.

"He thinks—" began Esteven.

"You, too," said Giles. "Be quiet. Now, Groce, let's see this book."

Glaring at Esteven, Groce reached into a pocket of his coveralls and brought out a brown-covered volume almost small enough to be hidden in the closed hand. But when Giles took it and opened it, he saw that the little pages did, indeed, have a good deal of white space on them, between and around the blocks of printed diagrams.

"It's a math book all right," he said. "Propositional calculus, you said, Groce?"

"That's right, Honor, sir," said Groce, somewhat less truculently. "My grandfather bought it, back before the Green Revolution. It's an heirloom—from the days when computes took up whole floors in buildings."

"A book two hundred and twenty-five years old?" Giles nodded. "I don't blame you for not wanting it damaged, Groce."

He frowned suddenly and took a corner of one page between his middle finger and thumb, rubbing it.

"It's in remarkably good shape for a book that old," he said. "How—"

"It's been plastic-injected. All the original materials have been replaced with single-molecule stuff," said Groce, proudly. "My father had it done. Cost him the equivalent of a full month's pay, but it hasn't shown a touch of wear since then, in fifty-four years."

"Plastic?"

The word came from Esteven, in an odd voice. He was staring at the book in Giles' hand.

"That's right, Esteven," Giles said. "That's what Groce just told us. What about it?"

"Why . . . nothing," said Esteven, still staring at the book. "I mean . . . I suppose if it's plastic my stylo wouldn't work on it. I wouldn't be able to use the pages to write on, anyway. . . ."

"Damned shame you didn't think to ask about that before you tried to steal it from me!" Groce spat at the other arbite.

"I did ask you for it first—"

"And I told you no!" shouted Groce. "Do I have to give reasons for not wanting to tear up an heirloom book?"

"It might have been a little wiser if you had," Giles said to him, dryly, handing back the book. "Here. Keep it someplace where no one can get at it to tear pages out, from now on."

He turned back into the front section of the ship and his own cot. Behind him the recorder started up, and the familiar three chords of Bosser, backing up the suggestive lyrics of the throaty Singh, followed him.

He sat down on his cot and discovered that Mara had followed him. She was standing over him.

"Yes?" he said, looking up at her.

"Could I show you something?" she asked. Her face was serious, almost grim.

"What is it?" he asked.

"If you'll come with me—"

A sudden new explosion of voices broke out in the middle section. The Bosser-Singh combination abruptly gave way to a solo instrument sounding a high-pitched bit of wailing melody. Giles shot up from his couch and strode into the middle section, to find Groce trying to tear the recorder out of Esteven's grasp.

"—and kill that kind of thing!" Groce was shouting. "Give us the Bosser and Singh back. That was good!"

"In a minute . . . just a minute," said Esteven, pleadingly. "Just listen a second to this spinny—"

"What d'you mean, spinny!" snarled Groce. "It's a lousy kilin, and I hate kilin music!"

"Sir?" Esteven appealed to Giles. "You know music, Honor, sir. You've probably had education in it. You can tell the difference, can't you?" Esteven's trembling fingers were snapping time to the music.

"That's right, it's a spinny," Giles said. "But I'm afraid music's not one of my larger interests, Esteven. The Bosser and Singh suits me as well as anything."

He started to move on, but Esteven held up a hand, asking him to wait a moment. Moved by an obscure sense of pity for the man, Giles did.

"I was right, though, sir," said Esteven. "You do know. You do understand. Would you be surprised if I told you the name of the soloist on that spinny? That's me. It's my job arranging and setting up pieces like that. I know I can just program an instrumental part and have it come out perfect from the synthesizer. But there's so few like me nowadays who really know and love their instruments—I always feel you put more into the recording if you have at least a part or two played like that—I mean, if you use a live musician—"

The music stopped suddenly as Groce reached out and stabbed the control button. Bosser and Singh poured forth.

Esteven opened his mouth as if to protest, then closed it silently.

"Groce," said Giles. Groce looked up at him. "That's Esteven's recorder, not yours. Just like your grandfather's book belongs to you, not him. If you don't like what's being played, come and tell me. I don't want you touching the recorder yourself again."

"Yes, sir," muttered Groce, looking down at his cot.

"Give them half an hour or so of what they want," Giles told Esteven, "then take half an hour to play what you want."

"Yes, Honor, sir," said Esteven. The look of gratitude in his eyes was so overwhelming as to be almost a little sickening. Giles turned to Mara, who was standing just behind him.

"Now," he said. "What was it?"

"If you'll come with me," she said.

She stepped past him and led the way into the rear section, which was empty at the moment. There, she turned to the nearer wall of the hull and the vine on it. She searched among the leaves for a moment, then lifted a stem of them out of the way with her left hand and pointed with her right forefinger.

"Look at this fruit," she said to Giles, in a low voice.

He stepped close to the vine and brought his gaze down to the fruit she indicated. At first he saw nothing about it that was different from the appearance of the other fruits he had been accustomed to seeing and eating. Then, shading his eyes against the dazzle of the eternal bright lights overhead, he began to make out faint shadows on the *ib* fruit's surface. He stepped closer and saw that the shadows were spots of darkness, seemingly just beneath the skin of the fruit.

"I've seen one or two fruit before like this," Mara was saying quietly in his ear. "But none of them had the number of brown spots this one has. When I ran across it, I did some more looking around the vine and found a couple of dozen of the fruit that have at least two or three brown spots like this."

"Could you show me some of the others?" he asked.

She nodded and led him down along the vine. With a little searching she uncovered three more fruits with a fair number of spots on them, though not as many as the first one she had shown him.

Giles turned back to examining the vine generally. Superficially, it looked very much the same as it always had been, but after a few moments he came across a leaf that was blackened and curled up. He broke it off thoughtfully, and went looking for more of the same.

He collected four such leaves, then went back to detach the first fruit Mara had shown him.

"I'll take these to the Captain," he said to her, and looked down at her with approval. "You were wise not to tell any of the others about this before telling me."

She gave him a faint, thin smile.

"Even an arbite has a touch of common sense, Honor, sir," she said.

He could not tell if she meant her tone to be mocking, or not.

"I'll let you know, of course," he said, "whatever I

learn from the Captain. I appreciate your coming and telling me about this. Meanwhile, keep it to yourself until I've talked to the Captain."

"Of course," she said.

He turned and left her, heading toward the front of the lifeship and holding the leaves and fruit hidden in his hands as he passed through the middle section. His mind was crawling with a vague uneasiness. Naturally, no system as simple as this could be expected to endure indefinitely. While the lifeships were unused aboard the spaceliner, the nutrient tank would have to be added to at intervals to keep the vine alive and operating. No system was perfect. But his researches back on Earth had told him that it should be good, with the lifeship carrying a full load of passengers, for six months at least. And those aboard here now were far from a full load. He stepped around the edge of the screen hiding the Captain.

Th alien officer was sitting in her command chair, her eyes closed.

"*Rayumung,*" said Giles, in Albenareth, "*I need to speak with you.*"

She did not answer; nor did she open her eyes. He went closer to her, to the very arm of her command chair. Now hidden himself deep behind the screen that protected her, he spoke again, no louder, but almost in the tiny dark orifice of the alien ear.

"*Captain! Captain Rayumung!*"

She stirred. Her eyes opened, her head turned, and she looked at him.

"*Yes?*" she said.

"*I need your attention to a matter,*" Giles said. "*It concerns the ib vine.*"

"*The vine is not to be disturbed. Take only the fruit as directed.*"

"*Rayumung,*" said Giles, "*is your memory failing you? You have never given us directions for using the fruit of the ib. I from my own knowledge informed my people.*"

"*As long as the knowledge has been made available. Act accordingly.*" The eyes in the dark and wrinkled face closed again.

"*I repeat,*" said Giles, more loudly. "*I must have your attention. There is an emergency about the vine.*"

"*Emergency?*" The eyes opened.

"*Will the Captain examine this fruit?*"

Giles held the fruit he carried, the one Mara had first shown him. The three long dark fingers of the alien's right hand reached out and took it in their tripodal grip. The Captain held the fruit for a moment, gazing at it, then returned it to Giles.

"Do not eat this. Dispose of it."

"Why? What's wrong with the fruit?"

"It will make you ill. Perhaps you will die. Do not eat such fruit."

"I did not need your advice to caution me about that," said Giles. *"I asked you what was wrong with it."*

"It is no longer wholesome."

"That, too, was obvious." Giles had made the mistake of losing his temper with the alien Captain before this. He told himself he would not make it again, now. His voice, in the buzzing Albenareth tones, was icy, but as controlled as the Captain's. *"Look at these leaves, then."*

He held out the four curled and darkened leaves to the Captain. She took them, held them as she had held the fruit, and passed them back.

"The leaves," she said, *"are dead."*

"I can see that," Giles said. *"I want to know why. Why are the leaves dead? Why is the fruit not wholesome, suddenly? What has gone wrong with the ib vine?"*

"I have no idea." The Captain's voice was distant, almost indifferent. *"I am a spaceship officer, not a biotechnician. There are those who could tell us what is wrong with the ib, but they are not here."*

"Have you no tests you can make? How about the nutrient solution from the converter? Can't you test that to see if there's anything wrong with it?"

"There is no testing apparatus on board this lifeship."

"Yes," said Giles, grimly. *"In fact, there is very little of anything aboard this lifeship. Like all your ships, Captain Rayumung, it is falling apart from old age and lack of proper maintenance."*

He had hoped to prod the Captain out of her strange condition of lassitude and into anger. But the attempt did not work.

"You do not understand," said the Captain, in the same distant voice. *"The ships are dying. The Albenareth are dying. But we do not die as lesser races do. We do not choose to curl in on ourselves and perish in the soup of an atmosphere, to be broken down chemically into the*

soil, and less than soil, from which we came. It is our choice to go proudly to meet our deaths, one by one, as the further Portal lets us pass, until the race of Albenareth are known no longer. You are an alien and do not understand. You will never understand. The ib vine on this lifeship, too, is dying—it does not matter why. Since you are dependent on it, you will die also. It is a matter of chemistry and physical law."

"What about your responsibility to your passengers?"

"I've told you," said the Captain, *"my responsibility is to deliver them—whether they are alive or dead at the delivery point does not matter."*

"I do not believe that," said Giles. *"When you took those of us aboard here, together with the rest of the human passengers who boarded your spaceship above Earth, your responsibility was not indifferent to whether they reached their destination alive or dead."*

"That was then," said the Captain, *"before some one or more of your humans destroyed my ship and cost all Albenareth aboard her great loss of honor. If human actions initiate a logic chain of actions that leads to human deaths, I am not responsible."*

"I do not agree with you," said Giles. *"And in my case, as I have told you, I am responsible for the lives of my fellows aboard. You may be able to excuse your actions to yourself, but I warn you, neither I nor any other humans will excuse them—and your race needs the payments in metal and energy my race gives yours, if you want to keep these ships of yours running for the next few thousand years—or however long it will take you all to die properly."*

"I will not argue with you," said the Captain. *"What eventuates from the arrival of you humans at Belben, dead or alive, must be the concern of others of my race. It is no longer mine."*

"No longer—" Giles broke off, at the stab of a sudden, sharp suspicion. *"Rayumung, is it that you, yourself, don't expect to reach Belben alive?"*

"That is correct. I will not."

Giles stared down at the long, narrow, dark figure in the command chair.

"Why?" he snapped.

The Captain looked away from him, transferring her gaze to the nearer of the two screens on the control console before her—a screen showing the endless darkness of space sprinkled with star lights out ahead of the lifeship.

"*The ib vine does not have the nutrients I now require,*" she said. "*Alone, it would nourish me as long as necessary for survival. But I am no longer alone. I carry new life within me—a new life, as yet free of any taint of dishonor, to keep alive the search for whoever destroyed my ship. A new life, if necessary, to found a family line which will never cease from searching until the truth is known. It is a ship's life, bred of the Engineer and myself, but carrying the honor line of all my officers and crew who were with me while my ship lived. I will die, but my ship's child will take what it needs from my body and live to land at Belben, to become a ship's officer and erase the shame of what has happened.*"

She fell silent. For a long moment, Giles himself had no words. All at once it leaped into context in his mind—the elastic ties around the limbs of the spacesuit of the Engineer, that could do next to nothing to protect that alien's life in case of leaks, but which could protect the vital generative area of his central body against the dangers of decompression. That—and what it was that Di had seen, there in the alien blood-marked back of the ship when she had wandered in on the Captain and the dying Engineer.

"*But you could have lived if you hadn't done . . . this,*" he said. "*Why didn't you just survive, yourself, in order to do your own erasing of the shame of what's happened?*"

"*I am already dishonored beyond the cooperation of any but members of my own ship's company, all of whom now are dead. But the new life within me, being stainless, cannot be denied cooperation by another Albenareth without new reason; and that assistance will be needed to find whoever destroyed my ship.*"

There was another pause between them.

"*Very well,*" said Giles, finally. "*I am not Albenareth, as you say, and I admit I do not fully understand. But I still see no reason why you will not change the course of this lifeship to 20B-40 and give the rest of us a chance of life. In fact, now I formally insist that you change course.*"

"*No,*" said the Captain, emotionlessly. "*The life that I carry will be stainless at birth, but more than this is needed. There must be some inherited honor for the young one to ensure its chance at the rank and duty of a ship's*

officer, which is available to a few, even among the Al-
benareth. If this lifeship delivers what is left of its pas-
sengers to Belben, alive or dead, there is that honor.
Otherwise, there is only expediency."

"There's no honor in saving lives?" snapped Giles.

"How could there be?" said the Captain. *"A life saved*
by other than that life's owner has only been intruded
upon, in its own area of honor—its own responsibility to
delay as long as possible the satisfaction of passing through
the further Portal. Also, these are only human lives. If
you and your people were Albenareth, you would all gain
honor by joining me in the execution of my duty, which
is to convey them to Belben. As you are not, it makes no
difference one way or another. But Adelman, it is to
Belben we go and no other destination."

The Captain closed her eyes.

"Rayumung . . ." said Giles.

The dark figure did not answer. Giles turned and walked
out, leaving the motionless alien behind him.

In the first section of the ship he saw Hem lying on his
cot and Mara standing as if waiting. For a second he stared
at her, puzzled. Then, with a jolt, memory returned. He
had become so involved in his conversation with the
Captain he had forgotten that they had been speaking the
alien tongue, which Mara of course did not know.

He smiled at her, now, to reassure her.

"I'm afraid," he said, "the Captain doesn't know much
more about the vine than we do. It's not the Captain's area
of specialty. So, for the present, we'll simply avoid any of
the spotted fruit. If you find any like that, pick it and
put it directly into the converter. Will you tell the rest
about that?"

"Yes," she said. She did not turn away immediately,
however, and it seemed to him that she was watching him
a little curiously. "That was all you were able to find out,
in spite of talking to him so long?"

"The Captain and I always seem to have a bit of an
argument whenever we talk," he said. "I'm afraid I didn't
learn anything else worth telling you. But I'll be talking to
the Captain again, and as soon as I have some information
to pass on, I'll pass it on. But for now, just avoid the
spotted fruit as I said, and don't worry. Tell the others
that."

"I will," she said.

She turned and went back into the middle section of the ship and he heard her voice, although, with the recorder running in the background, as it was more and more constantly now, he could not make out exactly what she was saying to the rest. Gradually, the sound of the recorder was coming to be used as a privacy tool, and as such it was welcome.

Giles lay down on his cot and gave his thoughts over to the problem of the Captain. One way or another, their course must be changed to the destination of 20B-40—and the change must be made while the Captain was physically still able to make it.

Sixth day—23:57 hours

The humans, except Giles, were all asleep. Although the lights still blazed eternally overhead, they had all fallen into a pattern, a sleeping and waking cycle. At about midnight, lifeship-time, Giles sat murmuring into the recorder to log the day before trying to sleep himself.

"Sixth day," he dictated. *"There's still enough fruit, but the numbers of those with spots are increasing. More leaves dying. Morale, about the same. This is the end of the sixth day."*

He put the recorder safely away on the floor at the head of his cot, where Esteven could come and get it in the morning, and reached for the sleeve he had cut from his shipsuit. The orange-colored sleeve, from wrist to shoulder, was long enough to make a workable blindfold with its two ends tied behind his head—enough to keep the light out so that he could sleep more easily. He had no way aboard the lifeship of seeing himself reflected, but he could imagine how his one bare, exercise-muscled arm and his curly, six-day beard gave him a wild, almost barbaric look. Curiously, none of the arbites had such a look. Though Groce and Esteven both were sprouting considerable beards—touched with a few gray hairs in Groce's case—they looked disheveled and unwashed, rather than wild. Frenco and Hem, on the other hand, had no beards to speak of. Frenco's consisted of a few limp black hairs scattered sparsely over his lower features. Hem had a faint fluff of blond mustache and some sandy stubble following the line of his jawbone on each side from chin to upper cheeks.

Nearly all of them now, except Biset, had sacrificed at least a small part of their clothing to make a light shield for their eyes during sleeping hours. He could hear them breathing slumberously beyond the screen now. Luckily none of them was a snorer of any heaviness or regularity, although Hem occasionally rolled over on his back and fell into a sort of deep rumbling in his throat.

Giles wrapped his loose sleeve around his head and tied it, then stretched out on his cot. He waited for sleep, but it was slow in coming. At moments like this he became actively conscious of the closeness of the surroundings, the thickness of the atmosphere, and all the unresolved problems that stood between them and a safe planetfall on 20B-40, to say nothing of those standing between him and the successful completion of his mission. He turned over restlessly on the cot, looking for a more comfortable position. Even assuming the *ib* vine held up and they could make the course change to 20B-40, could the arbites stand up to another thirty or forty more days like this?

Something intruded on his thoughts. Something barely heard, like a cry cut off before it had actually had time to clear the throat of the one crying out. He listened . . . but he heard nothing.

He continued to listen. There was no sound but the nighttime heavy breathing; even Hem's approximation of a snore was silent. And in addition to those noises there was nothing . . . or was there?

He sat up on the cot, pulling the sleeve from his head. The bright light overhead burst on his eyes in its full strength. Through the dazzle of it as his vision adjusted, he identified what he thought he had been hearing—a quiet thudding from the very bow of the ship.

He got to his feet, his sight clearing. The quiet thudding was coming from behind the screen that hid the control console of the lifeship and the Albenareth Captain. He stepped forward, turned the end of the screen—and saw the alien choking the life out of Esteven. The man's face was dark, his hands plucking feebly at the alien fingers fastened with casual power around his throat, his kicking heels making the almost inaudible noise Giles had heard as they drummed upon the fabric-covered flooring.

Giles threw himself at the Captain.

"*Release him!*" he shouted in Albenareth, tearing at the Captain's fingers. It was like trying to pull steel rods loose. "*Let that man go! You're killing him!*"

"*I am in process of disposing of him,*" said the Captain coldly, continuing to choke the entertaincom. "*He has profaned the book of navigation and should be removed from our midst in the interest of honor.*"

"*You do yourself dishonor!*" raved Giles. "*He is not yours to dispose of. You take something to which you have no right! He is my man—mine to keep or mine to kill—not yours! You are a thief, without honor!*"

The reaction was instantaneous. The Captain literally dropped Esteven, who fell gasping to the floor. The Captain's hands were up, her long fingers now directed toward Giles, who braced himself to face attack by the alien.

But the hands dropped. The Captain turned from Giles and dropped into her command chair, to gaze at the forward screen.

"*Take him, then.*" The Albenareth's voice was cold and indifferent. "*He has dared to touch and turn the pages of our Holy of Holies. But do with him what you want. Only, if I see him in the forward part of the lifeship again, I will consider that one who cannot control his property lies about his rights to it.*"

Giles pulled Esteven to his feet, lifting him bodily into the air, slapping aside the feeble efforts of his hands when the entertaincom tried to resist, then shoved the man ahead of him, out of the Captain's area, through the first section of the lifeship and into the middle section.

The other arbites had crowded into the first section, awakened by the sound of the loud voices in Albenareth. They rolled back now like retreating surf before the approach of Giles with Esteven, into the middle section. When Giles with the other man had joined them there, he shoved Esteven into their arms, beckoning Mara to him. She hesitated, and in exasperation he reached out a long arm and literally hauled her close enough to him so that he could speak to her in tones too low to be heard by the Captain up front.

"Take care of Esteven," he told her. "The Captain was choking him, but he'll be all right."

"What—" began Biset, demandingly. Giles stopped her with a glare.

"I've just saved his stupid life—keep your voice down!" whispered Giles harshly. "And I don't guarantee to be able to save any more of your lives, unless you follow orders. Now, do what I say, and don't let Esteven beyond that screen there into the front of the ship if you value his life!"

He let her go and turned away. Behind him, Esteven had slumped down on the floor and was sobbing.

"I didn't mean anything wrong. I couldn't sleep. I thought it was just a book—to read, to look at, you know. . . ."

Giles returned to the front section of the ship, followed by Hem.

"Hem," he said to the big arbite, "keep them back there. I've got to do some thinking."

Hem nodded and stood in the doorway. Giles threw himself down on his cot. Now, on top of everything else, he had the puzzle of Esteven. Not for a second did Giles believe that the entertaincom had merely wanted to look at the navigational book. And to actually step into the private area of the Captain would have taken courage Giles would have been ready to swear Esteven did not have. On the other hand, what could the entertaincom have been hoping to gain from getting at the book? The Albenareth mathematics would have meant nothing to him—and the navigational manual would have no white spaces such as Groce's antique math book had owned, on which Esteven could play at writing music.

The recorder had started up with the familiar Bosser and Singh in the middle section of the lifeship. The puzzles in Giles' mind seemed to go up and down, around and around, with the repetitive melody of the music. . . .

He woke suddenly to the awareness that he had dozed off. Hem was looming over his cot.

"Mara wants to talk to you, Honor, sir," Hem said.

"Oh?" Giles sat up, rubbing his eyes into the clear vision of full wakefulness. He became aware that Mara was standing in the entrance through the screen as if before an invisible barrier.

"Sit down," he told her, motioning to the end of his cot. "Save your strength. We all need to save what strength we've got."

She hesitated for perhaps a second. He could not tell. Then she sat.

"You're right, of course," she said.

He smiled. It was one of the unlikely sort of things she had a habit of saying—certain statements or questions that, if they had not been said so innocently, would have been impudent. It was not up to an arbite like herself to pass judgment on the correctness of what he said. He remembered what he had thought of her shortly after he had first noticed her.

"Tell me, Mara," he said. "You didn't happen to grow up in the household of some Adelborn family, did you?"

"Did I?" She laughed. "Far from it. My father died when I was only three. There were eight children in our family—a computer error gave my parents a permit for that many offspring, and they didn't realize it was an error until too late. Then, as I say my father died, and my mother got special permission to devote all her time to bringing up her family—she even got permission to move my grandmother in, to help. So I actually grew up almost as if I'd lived a hundred and fifty years ago, before the Green Revolution."

He gazed at her, surprised.

"Weren't you enclassed?" he asked.

"Oh, I had to take the usual courses," she said. "But with a family as large as ours, whenever I was home we were in an environment of our own making. A regular old medieval family-type environment."

"Yes," he said. He felt a terrible pity for her. No wonder a girl like this could fall into the trap of joining an organization like Black Thursday. For a second he was almost tempted to warn her that Biset had identified her as a revolutionary. But the habit of duty silenced him.

"What was it you wanted to talk to me about?" he asked.

She glanced at the entrance to the middle section of the lifeship, but the recorder was putting out enough sound there so that she did not have to lower her voice unduly to speak privately to him.

"It's about Esteven," she said. "I thought you'd want to know. I'm not a licensed nurse, but when I was in secondary school I put in a year full time as a probationer in the medical services. I had the usual courses. There's something wrong with Esteven physically. His hands are ice-cold—here in this thick steambath air of a lifeship—and his pulse is rapid and erratic."

He looked at her with respect.

"That's good—your noticing that and coming to tell me about it," he said. "I don't suppose you've got any idea what could be causing symptoms like that?"

She shook her head.

"As I say," Mara said, "I was only a part-time volunteer worker for a year, and back when I was hardly grown, at that."

Giles nodded.

"Of course," he said. "Well, it's something I'm glad to know about. I'll try talking to Esteven himself and see if he knows what's wrong with him."

"Not that we can do much about it, whatever it is," Mara said. "Here on this alien lifeship with no medical equipment or drugs. I don't know what to do."

She sounded to Giles' ears to be genuinely upset.

"It's not your responsibility to do anything," he reminded her gently. "I'm the one who's responsible."

"Oh yes," she said, waving one hand as if to brush that statement aside. "You're an Adelman and you think you ought to take everything on your own shoulders. But you're stuck here with a bunch or arbites; and what do you know about arbites?"

"What do I—" he began to repeat in astonishment, and checked himself, hearing the long-ago echo of Paul Oca's voice saying almost the same thing to him. The astonishment carried him past what would have been an ordinary, instinctive refusal to discuss such a ridiculous charge with her. "Aren't you the arbite who told me how all the lower classes dreamed of a chance to go indent to one of the Colony Worlds—"

He broke off and glanced over at the other cot in the front section of the ship. But Hem was not there, nor was he in view in the middle section. Hem did not spend much time in the middle section anyway. If he was not up front, he was probably back harvesting the vine or collecting the fruit he would eat himself. Nonetheless Giles lowered his voice.

"Just the other day," he went on, "I had a long talk with Hem. Hem's miserable at being shipped away from the work-mates he used to know. He'd give anything to go back to Earth. Perhaps I know more about arbites than you think."

"Oh, Hem!" said Mara. "It's immoral, the way poor,

helpless children like him are gene-controlled to grow up as hardly anything more than animals—"

"Shh!" he said, genuinely alarmed for her. "Keep your voice down. "There's . . . someone aboard here might decide to report you."

Mara did lower her voice, but the tone of it was still scornful.

"You mean the split?" she said. "I'm not afraid of her!"

"Split?" he echoed.

"The Police agent," said Mara. "Biset."

He studied her, unable to believe it. "You . . . already know she belongs to the Police?"

"Of course," said Mara. "Everybody on the spaceship knew it. There's always one. The World Police sent an agent out with every shipment of indents. Any arbite knows that."

"What else do you know about her?" he asked.

"I know she's likely to report anyone she doesn't like, whether they've done anything or not. If she decides she doesn't like me she'll dream up some reason to report me."

He gazed at her gravely.

"The possibility doesn't seem to worry you much," he said.

"The word is they don't pay too much attention to Police agents like her out on the Colony Worlds when they turn in bad-conduct or revolutionary-talk reports and minor charges like that," she answered. "They've had too many Police agents coming out with shipments and trying to cause trouble before they're shipped back to Earth again."

"I think her accusation might be a little more serious than that." Suddenly Giles threw his sense of duty to the winds. Bisets were a dime a dozen. This girl, with her straightforwardness and courage, was a jewel among the stones of the gravel pile that was the arbite lower class. "She might accuse you of being one of the Black Thursday revolutionaries."

She looked at him.

"Oh?" Mara said.

Without warning, an invisible barrier had raised itself between them. They were no longer two people sitting together; they were opponents facing each other across a strip of disputed territory. Giles felt a powerful urge to break down and do away with whatever was separating them—an urge, the powerfulness of which surprised him.

But he had no time to examine the emotional angle of the situation now.

"She told me so," Giles said. "I didn't really believe it."

"That's good of you, Honor, sir," said Mara. "Of course, you're right. I'm not."

"I didn't think so," said Giles.

But the barrier was still there, in place between them.

She got to her feet.

"Thank you for telling me, though, Adelman."

"Not at all," he said, formally, helplessly. "Thank you for telling me about Esteven."

"I wanted to help," she said.

She turned and walked out. He let her go. There was a strange anguish inside him, at seeing her leave like that. He could not understand what had gone wrong.

It was some hours later, when the recorder was playing loudly in the middle section, that he looked up to see Biset, this time, standing by his cot. She spoke to him without preamble, in Esperanto, as soon as his eyes were on her.

"Forgive me, Honor, sir," she said, with no tone of actual plea for forgiveness in her voice at all, *"but I'm afraid I have to speak to you. I've warned you once about the girl, Mara, and her revolutionary connections. I must remind you now that your rank doesn't exempt you from the authority of the Police. You've been giving this girl a good deal more license than you should."*

"She came to tell me about—" Giles broke off. He had been about to tell this woman how Mara had come to inform him about Esteven's possible illness, and then it dawned on him that he was condescending to explain himself to her. A cold fury erupted in him.

"Get out!" he snarled.

He rose to his feet on the physical impulse of his own rage, but by the time he was fully upright, Biset was gone. He felt the pounding of his own heartbeat, marking its pulse in the big artery under his chin.

He strode back through the screen entrance into the middle section of the lifeship and caught a glimpse of Biset in a corner, staring at him with widened, white-encircled eyes as he went by. Mara was not there. He stopped by the recorder long enough to turn it nearly to full volume with one twist of his fingers, then went on into the rear section. Di and Frenco were there, and so was Mara, picking spotted fruit from the vine and putting it into the converter.

"Leave us," snapped Giles to Di and Frenco. They stared at him and hurried to leave the rear section.

He was alone with Mara. She turned to stare at him, puzzledly, as he came up to her.

"Biset," he said. Standing face to face with her, inches apart, it was just possible to make himself heard over the sound of the recorder while speaking in a normal tone of voice. They were entirely private under the noise of the music. "She came to see me just now with the damned effrontery to suggest I shouldn't talk to you."

Mara opened her mouth.

"Perhaps—" she began in the same formal tone on which they had last parted, but then her face and voice changed to a tone and expression of concern. "Perhaps you shouldn't."

"I?" he said. "I'm Giles Ashad of *Steel*. Never mind that. There was something I should have mentioned to you. I should have told you that if Biset tries to make trouble for you—in any way—you come to me. I suspect she may try to accuse you of being the one who planted the bomb that blew up the spaceliner."

Mara stared at him.

"It actually *was* a bomb, then?" she said. "How can she or you or anyone be sure about that?"

"She can't," said Giles briefly. "I can. I was the one who planted it there." Giles teeth ground together at the memory. "It wasn't intended to hurt anyone, and it certainly wasn't intended to destroy the spaceliner. It was only supposed to damage it at a particular point on its trip, so that it would have to turn aside to the closest planetfall—a mining world called 20B-40—for repairs."

For a second she only stared at him.

"All those lives . . ." she said. Then she changed and came forward to put her hand on his arm. "But you said you didn't mean to hurt anyone. What went wrong?"

His jaw muscles ached. He was suddenly aware that his teeth were clenched together. He parted them with an effort.

"I don't know!" he said. "I suppose like a damn fool—the damn fool I was, and we all were—we underestimated how rotten with age one of these Albenarethian spacecraft are. The bulkhead that ought to have contained the explosion, back there among the cargo, must have split wide open and the fire started—you saw it."

Her grip on his arm increased. She stared up into his face.

"Why are you telling me all this?" she said.

He looked at her grimly for a moment.

"Perhaps," he said, slowly, "because I trust you. I don't know why—I couldn't explain to anyone why. But just now I suddenly began . . . Suddenly I had to tell someone, and you're the only one I could bring myself to open my mouth to."

He saw her looking at him now in a way no one had ever done before. It disturbed him and, in an odd way, made him feel humble. He had never suspected that a woman might look at him with just that look. There were things he found he wanted to say to her, but a lifetime of training and discipline closed his throat when he tried to utter them.

Clumsily, he patted the hand with which she was holding his arm, and turned away. She released her fingers, letting him go. He went back through the middle section of the lifeship, pausing for a second to turn the volume on the recorder down to its previous level. All the other arbites there were staring at him and among them was the face of Biset.

He ignored them, going on into the front section and lying down on his cot, on his back. Throwing the loose sleeve across his eyes, he abandoned himself to the privacy and loneliness of artificial darkness.

Di was crying. Sitting on her cot and crying. For a while after her experience with the Captain and the dying Engineer in the rear section of the lifeship, having one of the other women with her had comforted her. Then she had seemed to get better, and it was the presence of Frenco that soothed her when she woke from one of her nightmares. But lately, nothing helped. She cried frequently and could not say why.

"What can I do?" Frenco asked. He was standing with Giles and Mara in the rear section. Di had just thrust him away from her when he had tried to sit down beside her.

"I don't know," said Giles, thoughtfully, looking at the girl. "Obviously she needs medical help. Obviously none of us is equipped to give it to her. Don't blame yourself, Frenco—"

"It was my idea to apply for indent to a Colony World!" Frenco said wildly. "My idea. The odds were a thousand to one against our getting it, and when we did, we couldn't believe it, we were so happy. Now—"

"The word I used," said Giles, "was 'don't.' Don't blame yourself. This depression of Di's could have one of any number of causes. It could be a result of the food, or a result of the atmosphere aboard. It could be something generic in her that would have cropped up even back on Earth. But we'll stay with her and do what we can for her. Call me if there's any help I can give you."

"And call me," said Mara to the boy, "anytime I can help."

"Thank you," said Frenco. But he said it wearily, like someone who has worn out hope.

"Brace up!" Giles said to him, sharply. It was the same hard, sensible advice he would have given another Adelborn; but then Frenco cringed, and Giles remembered he was speaking to an arbite. He softened his voice. "If we can get her alive to planetfall she'll be all right in the long run."

"Yes, sir," said Frenco. He made an effort to put some life back into his words and some animation into his posture.

"That's right," said Giles. "Why don't you leave her to herself now? You can see she'd rather be left alone—and you could use some rest. Come up to the front section and take my cot for a while."

Frenco looked at him gratefully.

"Thank you, Honor, sir," he said. "But you're sure—you think I can't help her at all by being here even if she acts like she doesn't want me?"

"I'm sure," said Giles. "Everyone else on board here will be keeping an eye on her for you."

Frenco nodded.

"Yes," he said. "Thank you. Thank you all. . . . I guess I will go and lie down up front, just a bit."

He went out.

Giles turned his attention to Mara.

"Have you been eating?" he asked. "You look like you're losing weight."

She gave him a wraith of a smile.

"We're all losing weight," she said. "I don't see how we can last another eighty days to reach Belben, if we and the vine keep going downhill like this."

"Yes . . ." Giles felt the sudden ache in his jaws that signaled he was clamping his teeth together again too fiercely. The gesture was becoming a habit with him, lately.

"What is it?" Mara was looking at him.

"Something . . ." He looked at Di, but Di was beyond listening—lost in the dark night of her own misery and the sound of her own weeping, added to the music sounds from the recorder in the middle section, that would keep anyone else from overhearing. "You know I said the plan behind my bomb was to turn the spaceship aside to 20B-40?"

"I remember," she said.

"There was a critical period," he said, "a maximum number of ship-days during which such a change of direction would be practical. The period of days began the day the bomb went off. I've been counting the days since. We've got no less than six days. After that it'll be too late to change course. We might as well continue on to Belben."

Her eyes were big. Or perhaps it was just the new thinness of her face that made them seem so.

"How close is this 20B-40?"

"Now?" he said. "About thirty days away."

"But we could hold on another thirty days!" Mara said. "I don't understand—"

"The Captain's refused to change course from the one set for Belben," he said. "There's no use my trying to explain to you why. I don't really understand it myself. Just take my word for it that it has to do with honor in the way the aliens see it."

"But what's wrong with him? Certainly just honor—"

"It's not a 'him,'" Giles said. "That's something I've been keeping to myself from the first so as not to scare the arbites—" He broke off with a short, harsh laugh. "Do you know, I'm beginning to forget to think of you as an arbite? We're all getting down to a basic common label of 'human animal' on board this boat. . . . No, the Captain's a female. Not only that, she's pregnant. The Engineer was the male parent, just before he died; and it must have been their . . . mating that Di stumbled in on, back at that time she can't remember."

Mara drew a deep breath.

"Oh . . ." she said.

"The fact that the Captain is pregnant ties in somehow with the matter of Albenareth honor, in taking the lifeship to its original destination, even though all of us—and she, too—are going to die before we reach it."

"But if she dies, what about the—the child?"

"It won't die. It lives on her body, in some way." Giles waved the matter aside. Somehow, as with the matter of the bomb, he felt immeasurably better just from having been able to tell someone else about the Captain, her pregnancy, and 20B-40. "At any rate, what it all adds up to is that I've got to find some way of convincing the Captain she has to change course to 20B-40 inside of the next six ship-days."

Mara shook her head.

"I still don't understand," she said. "Why can't we just take over and make the course change ourselves? I know these aliens are awfully strong, but there's eight of us and only one of her."

He smiled at her a little sadly.

"Do you have any idea what changing course means?" he asked.

"No," she said, "to be honest, I don't. It's a matter of using the controls up front a certain way, isn't it? But didn't you have to study the Albenareth and their ships in order to figure when the bomb needed to be set off? So don't you know how to work their controls?"

"The controls are no problem," he said. "The problem is calculating a new course that will bring us to 20B-40 and figuring the changes in the present course that will put us on that new one."

"But there's Groce and his compute," Mara said. "Groce could help you with any figuring you needed to do—"

She broke off at the shaking of his head.

"Why not?" she asked.

"I'm sorry," he said. "But you really don't have any comprehension of what's involved in interstellar navigation. The manipulation of the controls is simple, and the mathematics of course calculation can be performed by Groce's compute, all right. But navigation out here between the stars is a science by itself. It calls for a mind trained in that science, and preferably one that's already done some navigation."

"But what about you? You're an Adelborn, and lots of them have yachts they pilot themselves between Earth and the other planetary bodies of the Solar System. Haven't you ever done anything like that before?"

"A few hundreds of times," he said. "But interplanetary yachts like the one I had are preprogrammed with a great deal of information that out here would have to be worked out from scratch. The first problem in interstellar space is to find out where you are . . . and it builds from there. No, if the course change is going to be made, the Captain is going to have to be the one to do it, and she's going to have to do it while she's still alert enough to manage it. She's been getting less and less active, more and more withdrawn and indifferent, lately. I think from what she says it's that 'new life' she talks about inside her, draining the nutrients it needs from her."

Mara's jaw was at a stubborn angle.

"There must be some way," she said.

"No. It has to be the Captain. . . . Why don't you get some rest, yourself, and leave me to work with the problem?"

"I can watch Di. That'll leave you free to think."

He shook his head again.

"Watching her doesn't interfere with my thinking," he said.

She got to her feet slowly.

"Call me, though," she said, "the minute you need help."

"I will."

He watched her go through the entrance in the rear screen, into the middle section and out of sight. There was a weariness inside him that tempted him strongly to lie down, to stretch out horizontally, if only for a few minutes, but he knew better than to give in to it. Flat on his back, he would not be able to resist the desire for sleep that lately seemed to be plucking at his sleeve most of the time.

He must keep his mind alert and on the problem. There was a solution to any reasonable situation. The Captain's objection to the course change was difficult only because it was involved with alien psychological and social factors. If there was only some way to give the Albenareth female what she wanted, without in any way sacrificing human lives or interfering with his own duty . . .

He came awake with a start, to the realization that someone was standing almost at his left elbow.

He turned to look. It was Esteven.

"Sir, sir . . ." Esteven's voice was hoarse. His face was gray and sweating under the merciless light from the overhead lamps.

"What is it?" demanded Giles.

"I . . ." The words seemed to take more effort to pronounce than Esteven had to give them. "I need help, sir. You . . . you will help, Honor, sir?"

"Of course, if I can," Giles said. "Sit down, man, before you fall down."

"No . . . no, thank you, Honor . . ." Esteven swayed. "I must have . . . It's just a request, a small one. But necessary. Indulge me, if you will, please, Adelman. You know I . . . the Captain . . ."

"What are you trying to tell me?" demanded Giles. "Pull yourself together. Talk plainly."

"It's just that I need . . . Do you, Honor, sir, have . . . a piece of paper . . . in your wallet, maybe?"

"Paper? No, I don't even have a pad or stylo—" Giles broke off, looking at the other man narrowly. "This isn't that music-writing you keep talking about, is it? Why—"

"No, sir! No, Honor, sir!" The denial was a cry from Esteven's colorless lips. "I can't explain. But I have to have some paper. Just to touch. Just to look at. Please, please . . ."

The real pain in Esteven's voice was undeniable. Instinctively, Giles began plunging his hands into the various pockets of his shipsuit. He came up with various odds and ends, but nothing made of paper. There was the warrant, of course, but that was of incalculable value. He must not let Esteven know about it. Paper was almost a collector's item, on Earth, at least, nowadays. Only on the Colony Worlds was there much paper manufactured. How Esteven expected Giles, here on this alien lifeship, in just the clothes he stood up in, to produce a collector's . . .

Of course! Giles dug out his identity card case from a right trouser pocket. Behind the card was a souvenir folded banknote issued sixty years before by a small African country, before the last of the independent currencies had been done away with in favor of the International Credit Standard. Esteven snatched at it, but Giles pulled it back from the other's trembling fingers.

"Wait a minute," said Giles, sharply. "You said you just wanted to look at it, to touch it."

"To feel . . . to hold. If I could just keep it a little . . ." Esteven's mouth was becoming wet at the corners from escaping saliva. His lower jaw was making odd, chewing motions. Giles stared at these things, at the popping eyes and the strange grayness of pallor on the man's face, and suddenly the truth jumped into the conscious area of his mind.

"Tonky!" Giles reacted instinctively, snatching the banknote back out of Esteven's reach, and the cry from Esteven at the loss was proof enough. "A tonky-chewer! I've heard about the drug—one of the pseudohallucinogens, isn't it? You take it and nothing seems real after a while. So that's what's been at you!"

"Honor, sir . . ." Esteven was trying to crawl over Giles, to get at the hand with which Giles held the banknote behind him. The entertaincom's chin was wet all over now with saliva. "Please . . . you don't know what it's like! Every little wrong sound hurts. It hurts to move, even . . ."

Giles shoved the man away. It was like shoving away a child. Esteven seemed strengthless. He tumbled back from the cot to the floor and crouched there, panting.

"Be sensible," said Giles, coldly, although inside him he was moved as much as he was sickened by the sight of the man in this state. "Even if I gave you this banknote, it'd only do you for one or two more doses and we've got weeks yet before we reach a planet where you could get more paper. And the tonk has to be taken with paper, doesn't it? It has to be buffered with some cellulose or else it can hit hard and kill you. How did you get started taking a poison like that in the first place?"

"What does an Adelman like you know?" Esteven almost screamed at him from the floor. "I can play thirty-two instruments, but who wants to listen, nowadays? So I'm an entertaincom. I arrange and play moron-tapes of moron-music to moron-arbites; and that's my life, all the life I have. All the life I'll ever have—on Earth or out on the colonies. Oh, please, just give me half of the paper . . . just a scrap of it to go with the bit of tonk I've got left."

"No."

Giles got to his feet, putting the banknote back into his pocket. "I can't help you to do that sort of damage to yourself. I won't help you. You're going to have to face life without the drug when it runs out, so face it now!"

He strode off, through the opening in the screen beside him, headed for the forward part of the lifeship, away from the mewling pleas of Esteven. Inside himself, it felt as if a huge, cruel hand had just gripped his intestines and twisted them. Everything that he had learned in those years of his growing up, everything that he had come to believe in, sickened at the thought of Esteven there, groveling on the floor and pleading for a scrap of paper. Giles choked, almost gagging. He could not crawl and whimper like that—no matter what any drug, man, or alien should do to him. Anything would be preferable to such a state.

He passed through to the forward part of the lifeship and began to pace back and forth. There was no end to problems. Now that he knew what was wrong with Esteven, it was necessary to decide what to do to help the man. Obviously Esteven was going to have to do without the drug—and, with luck, that would break him of his dependence on it. But he would undoubtedly need attention and care while he was going through his period of withdrawal. . . .

Giles frowned, trying to recall all he knew about the drug—one of the illegal toxics made and circulated in the arbite social ranks. It was, if he remembered rightly, a purely synthetic drug, originally developed as an aid to psychiatric treatment, before its dangerous and addictive side had been understood.

It was a complex, long-chain molecule that affected the nervous system directly, causing poisoning and death if it was not absorbed by the system slowly. It had an affinity for carbohydrates, and any of these slowed down its action if taken at the same time as a minute quantity of the drug in its gray, powder form. Plain cellulose in the form of paper was the most convenient and most effective carbohydrate to companion a dose. Tonk, taken and chewed slowly with paper, reacted with its molecules locking onto the carbohydrate molecules, and was absorbed by the body chemistry only very slowly, over a matter of hours or even a couple of days. That meant that a little of the drug must go a long way. It must also mean that the body of an addict ended up having some trace of the drug lingering in its system most of the time . . . and deterioration, both mental and physical, would be swift under those conditions.

The *ib* fruit was high in protein and low in carbohydrates. Those carbohydrates it did have were easily and quickly digestible, of little use in slowing down the effect of tonk taken with them. This explained Esteven's attempt on the navigation book earlier.The pages of that book were made of vegetable fiber—

A wailing sliced through his thoughts. He jerked his head up to stare through the opening in the nearer screen.

Esteven was coming toward the front of the lifeship, his mouth open with a long rope of saliva pendent from it, keening the sound Giles had just heard, over and over again, breaking off only to chew and swallow, and wail again. His hands were out in front of him, reaching blindly. Plainly, he neither heard nor saw Giles.

He's taken some of the drug, Giles thought, taken it raw.

Even as he was thinking this, he was on his feet and headed back through the middle section of the lifeship to meet Esteven.

"I'll help you," he called to the drugged man. "Hold on. We can do something."

Staring eyes in Esteven's face glared right through him. Giles reached the man, grabbed him by the shoulders, and hurled him backward. For a moment, Esteven resisted with a strength that was unbelievable. Then he staggered back through the screen and against the *ib* fruit press. His outflung hand closed on the handle of the press, jerked at it, and the rust-eaten handle snapped off short, leaving a long length of it like a jagged-ended club in Esteven's hand.

He came forward again, still wailing, swinging the club with an overhand motion. Giles dived forward, trying to get under that swing, but he was only partly successful. The club glanced off the side of his head. Still struggling to keep his feet, he reeled sideways into a roaring red darkness on the very edge of unconsciousness.

Vaguely, he was conscious of Esteven going past him.

"Book . . ." croaked Giles to the other humans. "The navigation book! He's after it . . . stop him!"

His head was clearing now. But he saw the arbites of the middle section making no effort to stop Esteven. Instead they were scrambling out of his path, trying to stay as far away from him as possible. Giles got his half-stumbling body under control and lurched after the madman.

Hem appeared in the opening of the first screen. Esteven swung the club again, and Hem made a heavy, grunting noise, as the metal length thudded against his right upper arm, knocking him aside. Beyond Hem and in front of the book on its jewel-bright stand appeared the tall, lean, dark figure of the Captain.

"No, Esteven!" cried Giles, plunging forward. But he could not catch up with the man before Esteven reached the alien figure barring his way. A third time Esteven struck with the club.

There was no room to dodge. A human could not have escaped being struck. But the Captain swayed, bending her body in a sudden and gracefully serpentine arc to one side, so that the club whistled by, missing her by inches. At the same time her right hand shot forward, not clutching, but striking, the three long fingers clustered together to form a solid-ended rod that drove into Esteven's chest.

The force of the blow knocked the human backward, off

his feet. He dropped the club and lay for a second, apparently fighting for breath. Then he managed another choked wail and scrambled to his feet. Obviously, he had been hurt, at least the breath knocked out of him and possibly ribs were broken; but under the influence of the drug he was still moving. He lurched once more blindly toward the navigation book.

The Captain was waiting for him. But before he could reach the alien, who still stood barring the way, Giles caught up with him from behind, caught him around the body, and hurled him off his feet. The Captain stepped forward, but now it was Giles who barred the way.

"No!" shouted Giles, in Basic. He switched to Albenareth. *"I forbid it! He doesn't know what he's doing!"*

"This time I end him," said the Captain. She faced Giles and her powerful club of fingers were aimed at him now. *"I gave you warning."*

Esteven was starting to scramble up from the floor, but now Hem was looming over him. Hem raised his left arm, the heavy fist at the end of it balled into a rocklike shape aimed to descend on the nape of Esteven's neck.

"Don't kill him!" Giles shouted at Hem.

The blow from the big arbite was already started. Somehow, he managed to turn it slightly off target. It hit high on the back of Esteven's head, instead of in the vulnerable spinal area.

Giles turned back to the Captain, just as she started to brush him aside. *"No! Wait. Think. You are more powerful than any one of us, but what of all of us, together? If you have no fear for yourself, what of the new life you carry in you? Will you risk what all of us together might be able to do to it?"*

The Captain checked herself, inhumanly, in mid-motion, and was suddenly as still as if she had never intended to move.

"I know his sickness now," said Giles, swiftly. *"I did not before. Now I can guarantee he will not come forward in the lifeship or threaten to touch your book."*

Still, the Captain did not move. The adrenaline that had kept Giles on his feet since he had been hit on the head by the metal handle was beginning to die within him. He felt consciousness seeping out of him.

"Believe me!" he said urgently. *"It is one or the other. I will not let you kill one of my people!"*

For a second Esteven's life, and perhaps the lives of all the rest of them, hung balanced. Giles forced himself to stand upright, to stare into the Captain's dark, unreadable eyes. Within he prayed that the Albenareth would not realize how badly Giles, himself, was hurt, how Hem was one-armed now, how the other arbites would be like rabbits facing a wolf without Hem or himself to spear-head an attack.

"*Very well,*" said the Captain, stepping back. "*This last time I give you the life of this one. No more.*"

She turned and went in behind her screen, disappearing. Giles turned, fainting, to find himself caught by half a dozen hands, Mara's and Biset's among them.

10

"Feeling any better?" Mara asked.

"I suppose so," said Giles—then reproved himself silently for giving such a grudging answer. "Nonsense. I'm a lot better. Fine, in fact."

"Not fine," said Mara, looking at him keenly. "I know better than that. But you're going to live, anyway."

"Live? Of course I'll live. Why wouldn't I?" he said stiffly.

"Because you probably had a concussion," she said. "When metal and bone come together, it isn't the metal that gives."

"Well, never mind that," said Giles. He touched his hand to his bandaged head, pleased in spite of himself by the fact someone cared how he felt. "I have to admit things have been kind of hazy of late. How long was I . . ."

He fumbled for a suitable word.

"How long have you been like this?" she said. "Five days."

"Five days?" He stared at her. "Not *five* days?"

"Five," she said, grimly.

He was beginning to feel the effort of talking. He lay still for a second, while she did something or other down near the foot of the cot he was lying on.

"This isn't my cot!" he said suddenly, trying to sit up. She pushed him back down. He was in the rear section of the lifeship.

"Rest," she said. "Lie still. We brought you in here be-

110

cause we didn't want the Captain to see how helpless you were."

"Good," he said, staring at the lights overhead. "That was wise."

"Sensible."

"All right—sensible." He began to remember things. "How's Hem?"

"All right," she said.

"His arm wasn't broken? I was afraid."

"No. Just bruised. He's got bones like a horse."

Giles sighed with relief.

"Esteven—"

"Two broken ribs, I think. We had to tie him up for a day or two, while he went through withdrawal from the drug," Mara said. She came up near the head of his cot and handed him what seemed to be a small plastic envelope with a few tablespoonfuls of gray powder in it. "This is what's left of his tonk. We thought you'd want to be the one to keep it."

He took the envelope in a hand that required a surprising amount of energy for him to lift, and tucked the drug remnant away into a chest pocket of his shipsuit.

"You had to tie him up?" Giles asked. "But how is he now?"

"Quiet," she said. "Too quiet. We have to watch him all the time. He's tried to kill himself several times. They go into that sort of depression during withdrawal after the pains quit, Biset says. She's seen other cases of addicts arrested by the police and having to quit cold, like this. The depression can last for weeks. She also said we'd all be better off if he killed himself."

Giles shook his head, feebly.

"Poor lad," he said.

"He's not a 'lad' and he's not 'poor'!" said Mara sharply. "He's a very unhappy, maybe psychotic, full-grown man, who indulged himself in drugs and nearly got us all killed."

He stared up at her, puzzled.

"I had the wrong choice of words, I guess," he said. "But I don't understand—"

"No," she said. "That's your trouble. You *don't* understand!"

She turned and went off. He had an impulse to rise from the cot and follow her, to make her explain herself. But the first attempt to sit up made his head swim. He lay back, furious at his own helplessness, but helpless none the less.

He fell asleep. Later, he woke when it was evidently a sleep period for the rest of them. The recorder was turned down to a murmur, and there was no noise of human voices talking in the background. He felt much more clear-headed and comfortable.

He looked around him. He was alone in the rear section of the lifeship. It was as it had been. Even the broken handle to the press was welded back into place. He wondered what had been used for this. Only Di and Frenco were not to be seen—they must have moved into one of the other sections. The thought that they might have moved out of consideration for him was oddly touching. Curious. Before he had left Earth on this mission, he would have simply taken it for granted that any arbites would move elsewhere to give him space to himself.

Paul Oca had been right—he had not understood arbites at all. At least, he had not understood them anywhere near as well as he understood them now, after living with a handful of them in these close quarters for fifteen days. On the other hand, Mara had just finished telling him he didn't understand, and no doubt—he grinned wryly in the emptiness of the rear section of the lifeship—that was true also.

But all such matters of understanding were beside the point. He had probably been a fool to risk his mission and his life by trying to save Esteven from the Captain. But at least he knew enough about himself now to realize that he was self-condemned to such foolishness in certain areas of behavior. It was strange . . . Mara had objected to his calling Esteven a "lad." He had used the word unthinkingly as any Adelborn might use it in such a situation. But of course Mara was right: Esteven was not a lad, although it was part of Adelborn attitude to think of the arbites as simpler, childlike individuals, limited by birth and training.

Curiously, at the moment, he found himself wondering if exactly the opposite was not true. The arbites aboard were anything but simple, non-mature people. In fact, with the possible exception of Di and Hem—and possibly not even them, come to think of it—they were not merely adults, but hardened adults, scarred and twisted by the lives they had led, to the point of having or lacking certain traits of character.

He, on the other hand . . . perhaps he was the immature specimen. Life had not operated upon him to make him what he was. What he was in character and reactions had been a suit of armor ready-made and waiting for him to put it on at so young an age that he had no real judgment about its worth. Since then, he had worn it unthinkingly. It was not until this trip off-Earth, with its mission, its burning spaceship, its lifeship, and its handful of shipwrecked arbites, that he had begun to feel differently about many things, and change inside his armor. What he had felt and the changes he had experienced had left him' adrift for the first time, at a loss to understand the rights and wrongs of matters he had always taken for granted.

He felt lost, now, and weak. There was a strange unhappiness in him he could not identify. As if he was lacking in something . . . something necessary. For a second he entertained the thought that it might be a simple physical thing he was feeling, the natural aftermath of the concussion from the blow on the head. But that seemed hardly likely. . . .

He shoved that whole question aside. There was something more important to think about. If he had been out of matters for as long as five days, it was only a matter of hours now until the lifeship would pass the point where changing course from Belben to make an earlier arrival at 20B-40 would be possible. They had reached the point where the Captain must make the change—without any more delay—and, for the first time, Giles felt he had found a way of convincing her to do it.

Now was an ideal time to talk to the Captain, with all the others asleep. A trifle gingerly, half expecting any sudden movement to wake the swimming head he had felt earlier when he tried to sit up, Giles lifted himself first to a sitting position on the edge of the bed, then slowly got to his feet. But his head stayed clear. He was conscious of a feeling of delicacy, as if he was made of glass above the shoulders and might shatter if jarred too abruptly, but other than that he felt as good as ever.

He walked slowly and carefully through the pair of screens and up to the front of the ship. As he went, he examined the *ib* vine he passed. The dead leaves were many now, and only an occasional unspotted fruit showed among the mere handful that seemed to be ripening. When he got to the front section, where his own cot was, he saw the tank that collected and held the juice from the *ib* fruit. It was now welded against the hull in a new position, just back of the Captain's screen. Only the Albenareth, herself, could have done that. Giles had not even been aware that there were tools aboard capable of removing and rewelding the tank in this new position.

He went around the screen that hid the Captain's control area. The alien sat as he had seen her last, in the furthest of the two command chairs. Her eyes were closed and she did not move, even when he came up against the other command chair with his knees and the chair rattled.

"*Captain,*" said Giles, in Albenareth.

There was no response. The long, dark figure did not stir.

"*Rayumung,*" said Giles, "*I must talk with you. We have reached a moment of decision.*"

There was still no reaction from the Captain.

"*If you do not wish to discuss this matter with me, I will act without discussion,*" said Giles.

Slowly, the round, dark eyes opened. Slowly, the head swiveled to face him.

"*You will not act in any way, Adelman.*" The buzzing alien voice was as expressionless as ever, but now there was something distant about it, as if the Captain spoke to him from a long way off. "*I am not yet helpless to control what is done on this lifeship.*"

"*No,*" said Giles. "*But each day you give more of your strength to the new life inside you. I believe you are weakening faster than we, who lose strength only because we lack adequate food and drink.*"

"*No,*" said the Captain. "*My strength is greater and will remain greater.*"

"*I will accept that if you say so,*" said Giles. "*It does not matter. All that matters is that very shortly it will be too late to alter course to 20B-40.*"

The dark eyes regarded him without moving for a long moment.

"*How do you know this?*" the Captain asked.

"*I know,*" said Giles. "*That is all that is important. It is even possible that I could change our course for 20B-40 myself—*"

"*No,*" said the Captain. For the first time Giles thought

he heard a faint trace of emotion in the Captain's voice. *"That is a lie you tell me. A foolish lie. You are helpless here in space like all your race."*

"Not all our race," said Giles. *"Some of us know how to guide ships between the stars. But you interrupted me. I was about to say that whether I could change the course for 20B-40 or not, I would not, for I respect such decisions as belonging to the officer in charge of any vessel in space."*

"Then respect the course which takes us now to Belben."

"I cannot," said Giles. *"As you have a responsibility to the single life you carry, I have a responsibility to the seven other human lives aboard."*

"The lives of slaves," said the Captain, *"are of no value."*

"They are not slaves."

"As I count, they are slaves, and worthless."

"As I count, they are men and women. They must survive. To ensure that they survive, I am ready to give the Captain what she wants."

"You?" The alien gaze did not move from Giles' face. *"You cannot give me back my honor."*

"Yes," said Giles, *"I can. I can identify for you the one who destroyed your spaceship. I can deliver that individual into your hands."*

"You . . ." The Captain surged up from her seat. *"You know who did it!"*

"Touch me—" said Giles, swiftly, for the long, thin hands were almost at his throat, *"touch me and I give you my promise, which is my contract, that you will never know."*

The Captain dropped back into her chair.

"Tell me," she said. *"For the honor of all those who worked my ship with me, for the honor of that which I carry within me—tell me, Adelman!"*

"I will tell you," said Giles. *"I will place the individual I name in your hands, and your hands alone, to do with as you will—once all the humans aboard here are safely down on 20B-40."*

"You would have me change course from that destination marked out by honor and duty!" said the Captain. *"You would hold back information until I have lost all hope of buying credit of honor for the unborn last of my line, until you are landed among other humans who will protect you, no matter what. You will cheat me, human!"*

The last words came out on a high note that was almost a cry.

"I will name and give you that individual I speak of— free from interference, to do with as you will," said Giles steadily. *"That is my promise, my word and my contract. Your people have done business with the Adelborn for some generations, Captain Rayumung. When did ever an Adelborn cheat one of you?"*

"It is true," said the Captain, looking into the front viewscreen before her as if she hoped to find some support and assurance there. *"The word of such as you has always been good, in my knowledge."*

She stopped speaking. Giles waited. There was no sound, in the small area behind the screen guarding the control consoles and the command chairs, but the sound of Giles' own breathing. Finally, the Captain stirred.

"I must take you at your word," said the Captain at last, once more speaking in that distant voice in which she had first answered Giles. *"If I did not, and you were honest, I would have compounded the dishonor now upon me and mine, by passing by an opportunity to regain the honor I have lost."*

Giles breathed out, softly. He had not realized that he had been inhaling and exhaling so shallowly—mere cupfuls of air from the upper part of his chest as he waited for the Captain to decide. She turned her head back to look at him now.

"I will make the first course change now, the second course change later," she said. *"The angle is not such that a single change is indicated. After I've made the first change we must stay twelve hours on that course before the second and final correction can be made."*

11

"I don't want," said Giles, "any of you to think the situation isn't still serious, because it is. We've got twenty-seven days yet, minimum, to survive on board this lifeship; and the *ib* vine, as you know, has been putting out less and less fruit, for reasons the Captain doesn't understand any more than we do. Something seems to be poisoning it. I'm not sure but what the Captain thinks that it's us— we humans—that are the poisonous element. But the important thing is we're facing a situation with less and less fruit. Now, we can do with a minimum of food for twenty-seven days if we have to—but that fruit juice is our only source of water. So keep that thought in your minds and try to get used to using as little liquid as possible."

Giles had gathered the arbites, even including Esteven, who was by now somewhat recovered, into the middle section of the lifeship to brief them. He had just finished telling them the truth about the Captain's sex and much of what had gone on between the Captain and himself in his efforts to get the course of the ship changed to 20B-40. They had listened in silence, except for a general murmur of excitement when he had explained that they might be getting to planetfall earlier than had been expected. But generally, they had reacted less than he had expected.

He was being forced to the conclusion that they had never really appreciated the danger of the situation they were in. If not, perhaps they did not understand, now. It

117

was a thought that gnawed at Giles as he looked about at them.

"You've followed what I said, have you?" he demanded sharply, looking around at them all. "You realize what we're up against? It's going to be a real test of will power and physical determination to survive. You've got to keep your spirits up and your exertions down. Now, you understand that, and the seriousness of the situation, even with this course change?"

There was a pause and then a mild murmur or agreement from them, interrupted by a small, but curious noise from the front of the lifeship, where the Captain was out of sight behind the control-area screen. It had been a sound almost like that of an Albenareth clearing her throat —almost as if the Captain had been listening to him from the bow, and now was politely signaling her desire to say something.

Giles looked toward the front. So did all the rest, but the noise was not repeated.

"What was that?" asked Mara.

"I don't know," Giles said. "It's about time for the Captain to be making the second course change to put us on target for 20B-40. Perhaps something's come up. . . ."

He got to his feet.

"Stay here," he said to them and went forward.

He reached the edge of the screen and stepped around it. The Albenareth navigation book had been rotated upon its stand so that its pages faced the closest command chair. In that chair the Captain sat, arms on the arm supports, back stiffly upright against the back of the chair, and her eyes closed.

"Captain Rayumung?" said Giles in Albenareth. *"Is there something of consequence—some problem?"*

There was no answer from the alien figure. No movement, no response of any kind.

"What is it, Captain? What's wrong?" Giles demanded.

There was still no answer. The Captain's mouth was slightly open, her breathing light, and her body utterly motionless. Giles reached out and gently lifted one of the dark eyelids. Beneath, the pupil of that eye was rolled up out of sight.

"What is it?" He heard the voice of Mara at his elbow, and turned. Against his order, they had all followed him forward and they stood now in semicircle, gazing at the Captain.

"She's unconscious," Giles answered. "I don't know why. Look at her, Mara. See if you can find any reason."

Mara pushed past him and felt for a pulse in the Captain's long wrist. After a moment, she abandoned that effort and lifted an eyelid as Giles had done. Then she ran her hands over the Captain's body, feeling here and there, until her fingers came to rest at last at the back of the Albenareth's neck, just below the bone of the round skull.

"I've found it," Mara said. "A pulse. Has anyone got a chrono? No? Groce, can't you give me a second count, somehow, out of that compute of yours?"

"Of course," said Groce. He punched controls on the compute and began counting out loud as he watched its display screen. "One . . . two . . . three . . ."

Mara let him count to thirty before she let go of the Captain's neck.

"All right," she said. "You can stop. Adelman—" She turned to Giles. "She's alive. But I can hardly believe it. Her heartbeat's only about sixteen counts per minute. Do you know if their pulses are naturally that much slower than ours?"

Giles shook his head. "I don't know. But I doubt they can be that slow. They don't live any longer than we do, and they're warm-blooded and just as active. Heartbeats that low from a normal resting pulse rate of around seventy, as in humans . . ." He searched his memory but couldn't come up with any exact comparisons. "At any rate, it sounds like the Captain's in a coma—or a state of hibernation, or something like that."

It was Biset who put into words the question that was in all their minds.

"Did the second change in course get made before she folded up?" Biset asked. "What do you think, Honor, sir?"

"I profoundly hope so," said Giles.

He looked around the control board, but to his human eye it held no information that would answer Biset's question.

"I'll study these control consoles," he said, "and see what I can figure out. There's no reason for us to assume the worst until we know for sure. The Captain particularly wanted to—" He checked himself. He had not told the

arbites, of course, of his offer to give up the one responsible for the bomb, once the lifeship made planetfall on
the mining world. "She had her own strong reasons for
wanting to get to 20B-40. This coma, or whatever it is,
may be a natural state with Albenareth, at a certain period,
when one of them is carrying young. She would have
known the collapse was coming and made sure she made
the second course correction before letting herself fold up
like this."

"And if she couldn't help it?" Mara asked.

"I'm sure she could," Giles said, stiffly. "Find a cot for
her and put her on it. Go on!" he snapped at them, angered
by their hesitation. "She won't poison you if you touch
her."

Goaded by his voice, Hem, Groce, Mara, and Biset
picked up the limp alien body and carried it away. Giles
went back to examining the control area.

Ignoring the fact that he did not understand much of
the instrumentation, he examined what there was to examine, item by item. It was all alien, but none of it was
totally unfamiliar. Many of the items were counterparts
of what he had seen in the control area of his own and
other space yachts; other instruments were understandable
in terms of his limited knowledge concerning interstellar
navigation. Still others—like the viewscreen—were obvious
appurtenances for this kind of craft. Regardless of how
familiar each item was, however, he gave it the same minute examination as if he had never seen anything resem-
bling it before.

He drew a blank.

Not only was there no sign of anything gone amiss—
there was no clear evidence whether the Captain had made
the second course change or not before lapsing into her
present state of unconsciousness.

He was about to turn away and give up for the moment
while he attacked the problem from the angle of pure
speculation and rationalization, when the navigation book
caught his eye.

If he could only understand the information contained
in it, he thought, he could probably zero in on the answers
he needed. It was impossible for him actually to understand it, of course—not merely because of the alien mathematics involved, but from the viewpoint of the whole system of navigation of which it was a part. But he glanced

at the pages of the book, anyway. Each page was a double column of short lines of what could best be described as squiggles—the sort of apparently meaningless marks that Arabic seems to be to untutored Western eyes.

Then he saw the raw edge of torn paper between the two open pages in the spread spine of the book.

He stopped and bent his head to look more closely.

There was no doubt of it. A page had been torn out of the book. Why would the Captain—

Esteven!

"Esteven!" roared Giles. "Come up here!"

There was a moment, and then Esteven appeared, pressed along—hustled along would perhaps be a better term, Giles thought—by the others. Giles let them crowd the man up to him, then he turned and pointed at the book.

"Esteven—" he began.

Esteven burst into tears, falling on his knees. He clutched Giles around the knees and clung to him. He was obviously trying to explain himself, but the explosion of his emotion made him impossible to understand.

Giles looked out over Esteven's head, at the others.

"I called for Esteven," he said. "Did I ask for the rest of you?"

Embarrassed, they backed off and disappeared through the opening in the first screen. He kept staring after them until they were all hidden from his gaze, then he reached down and lifted Esteven to his feet.

"Now tell me," he whispered. "When did you tear a page out of this book? While I was unconscious?"

"No . . . no . . ." sobbed Esteven. "It was before . . . long before. Back before the pru . . . the Captain caught me the first time. Believe me . . ." Esteven grasped Giles' arm frantically. "I'm not lying. I wouldn't lie to you. You saved my life three times. First by not letting the Captain kill me the two times she was going to, and then by helping me kick the tonk. I never believed anyone cared whether I lived or died. But you cared—and you didn't even know me, except that I was on this lifeship with you. I'd do anything for you. Believe me—I only took one page, a long time ago. Just one page . . ."

"All right," said Giles, embarrassed by the man's naked display of emotion but moved by him, nonetheless. "I believe you. Now, go back with the others, and don't tell them what I talked to you about. Don't tell them you ever took a page. Understand?"

"Thanks . . . thank you, Honor, sir." Esteven backed away, turned, and went.

Giles turned back to the book. There was a cold feeling in him. He thumbed through the pages preceding and following the one that had been torn out, trying to see if he could find any marks that could represent page numbers. There were no such marks, but in spite of that, his suspicions grew and grew until they were so close to certainty that he was half prepared when Mara spoke unexpectedly behind him.

"So that's why the Captain collapsed," Mara said, quietly, as if the information was not a matter of life or death, but only something out of which casual conversation was made. "She turned to the page needed to make the second course correction and found that Esteven had already eaten it."

He turned sharply.

"Don't assume—" he began, but she cut him off. For such a small girl, it was wonderful how she always appeared to be able to meet his eye on a dead level.

"We're not fools or innocents, Adelman," she said. "Please don't try to treat us as if we were."

He looked at her soberly.

"All right," he said. "You're very probably right. Esteven stole and used a page from this navigation book sometime before the Captain ever suspected him. And it may be that the page he took and ingested was the specific page that the Captain needed to make the second course change."

"Which means," she said, "that the second course change was never made; and, far from being headed for 20B-40, we aren't even headed for Belben. We're headed for nowhere."

"Yes," he said. "I think that's likely."

He stared at her.

"You take the news very well," he said. "In fact, Mara, you amaze me. You're standing up to most of the disasters of this voyage better than any of the arbite men aboard. The only one who comes close to you in that way is Biset— and she's a woman, too."

"Women," Mara said, "have always been the stronger sex, Adelman. Hadn't you heard that?"

"Yes, of course," he said. "But you're—" He caught

himself up short, but she finished the thought out loud for him.

"We're arbite women?" she said. "That doesn't make it less likely—it makes it more. When the men of an oppressed group are beaten down, that tends to make the women stronger, not weaker. 'Necessity makes them stronger."

He nodded, slowly.

"Sometime, when this is all over," he said, "perhaps we can argue about that. But right now and here neither one of us ought to be wasting strength on argument."

"What are we saving our strength for?"

"For . . ." He smiled, as grimly as she had smiled at him on occasion. "Mara, you may have given up. I haven't."

Her manner softened suddenly.

"Good," she said. "I knew you wouldn't. Then you actually will take over the piloting, and make the second course change to get us to 20B-40?"

"Take over the piloting?" Her casual assumption that he could, almost took his breath away. "I've tried to explain how that isn't possible."

"What else is there to do?" she asked. "If you haven't given up it's because you still think we can get to 20B-40. And if we're going to get there, who else is going to manage it?"

He laughed. It was a laugh so full of irony that it surprised even him. Whether it surprised Mara, he could not tell. He swung back around to look once more at the alien controls.

"All right!" he said. "Leave me alone for a while. Leave me alone here to study things; and if there's a miracle capable of being worked, I'll try it!"

12

"All right, Groce," said Giles. "I want you to sit there
and listen to me. And I mean *listen*. If you don't understand what I mean, tell me. Interrupt whatever I'm saying
and tell me right away. This isn't a situation where you
can—"

He checked himself, as he had come to do so much
lately. He had been about to warn Groce that this was
not the kind of work situation encountered on Earth where
it was safe to pretend understanding when understanding
was actually not there. Now, some new sensitivity stopped
him.

"This isn't," repeated Giles, "a situation where we can
take the chance that you and I don't understand each other.
You follow me on that?"

Groce nodded. The man's face was hardly different of
expression than Giles had ever seen it, but Giles felt a
sense of excitement rising almost like steam from the small
body in the command chair next to his.

"All right," said Giles. "Now, I do know the broad
outlines of what needs to be done. First, we have to establish where we are—what our position is as a moving point
along the line of our course. Then we have to establish
the position of the destination we want—again as a moving
point along the line of its course—and from this work out
the direction and angle of change we want in our present
course to take it toward that destination."

To his surprise, Groce nodded.

"Sounds simple," said the arbite.

"That's probably because I'm making it sound simple," said Giles, "so I can explain it. The fact is that it isn't that simple at all. For the Captain it was. She took observations with the equipment here, or a figure from her book, to locate her ultimate destination, then referred to the book in other ways I don't know anything about, in order to translate that information into heading and correction factors. I can make observations with the equipment—I can do that much. I can also set a heading and correction factor into the drive control. But the gap lies in what the book would have told the Captain. How do I derive correction figures from the position figures I get by observation?"

"Why the correction?" Groce asked.

"Because this lifeship's powered by a warp drive, like the Albenareth spaceship was," Giles said. "You can't feel it, but about once every eleven minutes the drive is kicking us into warp space and back out again. We cover immense distances of normal space every millisecond that we're in warp, but we don't keep moving there more than a few milliseconds because in warp our motion's got only an eighty percent possibility of being correct. You understand? We're going in the right direction only about eighty percent of the time. Given the proper correction factor, the lifeship's computer would keep recalculating our path back on target for our destination and putting us back on target for our destination. But even with this, if you could see us from the outside, it'd look like we were wobbling through space in a very erratic manner. Unless we can establish a correction factor, we'll have to stop and recalculate our position by hand, every time we go in and out of warp—several hundred times every ship-day—until we're inside the solar system of our destination planet, and it'll take us a thousand years to get there—a thousand years we haven't got."

Groce shook his head with continued and determined optimism.

"This compute of mine, and me," he said, "can give you any constant you need, if I've got the rest of the elements of the problem. How do we start?"

"We start," said Giles, grimly, "by my trying to apply interplanetary navigation to interstellar space. Basically, what we're up against is a problem in solid geometry, only with moving instead of fixed points. . . ."

He continued explaining. It was a curious situation. Essentially, before they could get to grips with their problem, they had to educate each other. Groce, Giles found, was number-minded rather than space-minded.

Giles had to search and struggle for ways of presenting the problem to Groce in math terms the arbite could understand and use.

"Look," said Giles, "visualize cutting a triangle out of cardboard, or something of that nature, and holding two points of it with thumb and finger."

He held up his thumb and middle finger to illustrate. Groce nodded, frowning.

"The point—the angle—" went on Giles, "that you aren't touching is free to rotate in a circle. You understand?"

Groce nodded.

"All right," said Giles. "Assume the two angles your fingers are touching represent known positions. Then your position—the angle you aren't touching—lies somewhere on that circle; and to pin it down to an exact location, you take a third known point and measure the angle between it and either of the first two."

"Ah!" said Groce, his face lighting. His fingers danced over the keys of his compute, in self-congratulation at his own understanding, as a musician might play his instrument in a like situation.

"The first three points," went on Giles, "need to be unique in appearance, outside the galaxy, and a comfortable distance from the galactic plane—you remember my explaning to you what the galactic plane was?"

"Yes," said Groce.

"All right, then. Three such suitable points might be S. Doradus, the nucleus of the Andromeda galaxy, and the nucleus of the Whirlpool nebula—that's M51 in Canes Venatici."

"I don't—" Groce began.

"That's right," said Giles. "You don't know anything about these names I'm mentioning. Don't let it bother you. The point is that they're outside the galaxy, out of the galactic plane, and recognizable from anywhere *in* our galaxy. What I want you to understand is how we use them to determine our position."

"I understand that," said Groce, vigorously. "Of course. It's just geometry, in three dimensions, like you said."

"Good," said Giles. "Then I'll go on. Now, using those reference points I just mentioned will just give us a general location in our galaxy, so general it very nearly includes the Solar System, Earth, Belben, and 20B-40 all at once. In practice, after getting our general position with these points from outside the galaxy, we'd have to consult star charts and pick three bright, known stars closer to us and refigure case, we don't need to do that. I studied the stellar neigh- to get a more precise location. But, as it happens in this borhood of our original route to Belben and I know roughly where we are in a general area."

Groce nodded. It did not occur to him, evidently, to ask why Giles should have gone to the trouble of studying the star maps and other necessary space navigational material.

"I also know the position of 20B-40, in reference to the area of space it inhabits, and the larger stars of its neigh- borhood," Giles went on. "So the only thing we need to discover is our own position right now, as precisely as possible, and the angle from that to 20B-40. We've only made the single course change at the captain's hands since we left the original route to Belben, and I'm betting that this involved a single phase shift. Consequently we shouldn't be more than one phase shift off our original line of travel and still in a stellar neighborhood where I can recognize the larger stars and other light sources visible in the screen there—"

He pointed.

"In fact," he said, "I do recognize them. So calculating our present position should be relatively simple. I can use the control section of this lifeship well enough to take angle readings on the three stars I've pointed out; and that gives us our location, from which we can figure the angle from our present direction or movement to 20B-40. Then we're ready to make a correctional phase shift."

"What about what you talked about earlier?" asked Groce. "Everything so far you've mentioned is simple. I could run the calculations on something like that in my sleep. But what about that correctional factor you men- tioned? Didn't you say we had only an eighty percent chance of moving correctly through warp space even after we shift the lifeship on a correct course?"

"That's it," said Giles. He sat back with a heavy exhalation of breath. "That's the real problem. The correction factor represents a tendency for the vessel to drift in warp space. The drift is different with every vessel and each separate course it takes. The Captain got it from her book. Somehow we've got to work it out for ourselves—that particular adjustment figure that applies to this lifeship and the unique course that exists from where we are at this moment to our destination of 20B-40."

"How?"

Giles sighed again.

"The only way I can think of," he said. "We've got to calculate our course, then shift and recalculate our new position, to see how far off we are when we come out of shift. We keep that up, shift after shift, until we accumulate enough data on the error per shift to guess at a constant correction factor. In other words, something that the lifeship would do automatically, every few minutes or so, we're going to have to do by hand over and over again, until we learn enough to estimate a correction factor."

Groce scratched his head.

"Well, Honor, sir," he said, "we might as well get started, I suppose."

They got started. Theoretically, Giles had told himself, it was just a matter of doing the necessary work, sticking to it until enough data could be accumulated. Sooner or later they would have it done. Then would come the unsure part—the guessing at a correction factor and, with it, worry. But up until that point things, he had imagined, should go with fair smoothness.

But they did not. For one thing, the *ib* vine had been becoming steadily less productive all the while, and this was now becoming a factor that influenced everyone aboard.

The tiny food ration per person that the vine produced seemed adequate; no one had any real appetite. But the amount of juice the pulp produced was now noticeably less than what they all would have preferred, even those who at first had found the juice sickly sweet and unsatisfying. Thirst ruled everything. There were always at least three or four of them awake at all times now, keeping a jealous watch on the fruit picked and on the juice container. Their skins were tight and shiny, their mouths always dry. They looked at one another with suspicion.

To complicate matters, there was the Captain, still lying

on the cot where they had put her, breathing so slowly it was hard to tell if she breathed at all, neither alive nor dead—but able to swallow automatically the daily ration of juice Giles insisted be given the alien along with everyone else. Mutterings about the waste of that ration of juice rose among the others and finally forced Giles to leave his calculations and face them all down.

"But why?" Di wailed. "She's not even human. And she's the one who got us in this fix! Anyway, she's probably already as good as dead—"

"She's alive!" snapped Giles. His own thirst had brought him close to the end of his tight-leashed temper. "If we refuse an Albenareth care in a situation like this it'll give the Albenareth an excuse to refuse care to humans if another situation like this ever happens and it's the Albenareth who've got the chance to keep the juice, or whatever's needed, for themselves. We've got a responsibility to treat this alien just exactly the way we'd want ourselves treated if it was the other way around."

"Damn the responsibility!" muttered a male voice. Giles looked about quickly and met the sullen eyes of Frenco, Groce, and Esteven. Only Hem returned his gaze without hint of mutiny.

"We won't damn responsibility or anything else," Giles said slowly, looking at each one of them in turn, "while I'm here. Is that clear?"

They made no sound. They were not yet ready to defy him face to face, but from then on, he made a point of breaking off work and watching when it came time for one of the others to lift the alien head and hold a partially filled cup of the precious juice to the unconscious lips. Twice he caught one of the men going through the motions with an empty cup. After that he gave himself the added task of actually bringing the juice to the Captain and getting it down her throat.

Meanwhile, even the calculations in which he and Groce were engaged did not go well. Under the nagging discomfort of his continual thirst, Giles blamed himself for not being more clearheaded when the first of the obviously wrong results showed up. Groce's compute, he reminded himself, was after all immune to thirst. He painstakingly recalculated with the other man's help, found a difference he was too weary to check out, and carried it through to a conclusion that appeared to check out.

But the same thing happened several times, and in a moment of fury he snapped at Groce, who exploded in denial.

"Wrong? How can I be wrong? I've never made a mistake. Never! It's your figures that're wrong—Honor, sir!"

The "Honor, sir" came out as an obvious, if not intentional, afterthought. Groce did not stop at that, but continued on for some seconds, in an injured tone of voice, reiterating over and over again how impossible a mistake was on the part of himself and his compute.

"All right, all right. I believe you," said Giles, finally. "Now, let's drop the subject and recalculate."

They did. But in spite of going over this particular calculation twice more, they still got a figure that was obviously wrong.

"We can't have moved that far on the last warp shift," muttered Giles. "That much of a shift would give us an error greater than our total progress. . . ." He made up his mind. "Groce, let me see that compute!"

Groce handed it to him reluctantly. Giles examined it, but could find nothing out of the ordinary about it. It was simply a sealed box with ranks of keys with either numbers or symbols on them. Even if he could open it up, he would not be able to tell if anything was wrong with its interior construction, and Groce knew no more about that than he did.

"All right," said Giles, handing the instrument back. "We'll do it once more, from the beginning, slowly, and double-check every step as we go."

They began the recheck. In spite of himself, Giles found he was watching each calculation Groce made with a sort of paranoid intensity. Many of the motions Groce's figures made on the buttons were meaningless to Giles, but when it came to the other man entering up the compute figures that Giles had just told him . . .

"*Groce!*" roared Giles, suddenly—and Groce's fingers checked abruptly on the keys as if arrested by a paralytic spasm. "Groce!" Giles' voice was lower now, but snarling. "Groce, that was a nine I just gave you. You punched a five."

Groce raised his eyes from the compute to Giles' face, the arbite's mouth open to protest. But no sound came forth. Seeing the expression of the other as a mirror to his own, Giles realized that there must be murder written on his own features. Words came softly, viciously, from his throat without his willing them.

"So," he said, "you never make a mistake, you and your compute? You never make a mistake . . ."

His voice was rising in spite of himself. A madness born of thirst and frustration was beating in a pulse at his throat. He was beginning to rise from his chair—when an unexpected hoarse shout in Hem's voice broke in on the mounting tide of his fury.

"Wrong!" Hem was shouting. "Let go—stand back. Honor, sir—come! Come quick!"

Giles bolted from his chair and brushed past Groce, who was in the outer of the two command chairs. He went with long strides back through the openings in the two screen partitions, to find all the others clustered around the cot where the long, dark body of the Captain lay. Hem was holding Biset by the shoulder with one massive hand. His other was clenched in a fist with which he was warning the others back.

"Honor, sir!" he said, his face lighting up with relief as he saw Giles. "I knew you wouldn't want them to. I told them you wouldn't. But she went ahead anyway—"

He gestured toward Biset with his fist. The Policewoman met Giles' eye fiercely and without fear.

"That," said Biset, nodding at the silent shape of the Captain, "is a threat to all our lives. I was going to put her out of her misery." Biset looked down at the torn-off sleeve of an arbite shipsuit that half covered the Captain's mouth and nose.

"I don't know that she's in any misery. Neither do you," said Giles, harshly. "In any case, it's not up to you—any of you—to do anything about it."

He looked around at the rest of them. They all but glared back. Even Mara's face was still and set.

"You, too?" he said to Mara.

"Me, too," she said, clearly. "I wouldn't have done it myself, but I can't stand in the way of people who want to live. This isn't earth, Adelman. This is a lifeship lost somewhere in space with humans on board it who didn't ask to be here, and who've got a right to live."

Her steady look accused him of the bomb he had set aboard the lifeship—the bomb that had resulted in their all becoming castaways between the stars. For a second, grimly, he wondered what they would say if they knew that he had given his word to the Captain—a word he knew he would honor whether the Captain lived or not— to give himself up as the price of getting them all to 20B-40. But of course whatever reaction Mara and the others might have did not matter. He could no more tell them what he had done in an effort to buy their cooperation than he could break the word he had given. He was locked, lonely in the armor of his upbringing.

"Right or no right," he said, "no one, human or alien, is going to be killed aboard this lifeship while I can stop it. Hem, carry the Captain to my cot in the front of the ship, and watch her from now on. If you have to leave her, call me. As for the rest of you—if I find her hurt or dead, the one who did it will lose his own juice ration. If I can't find out who did it, I promise you on my word as an Adelman that I'll take the juice she would have gotten, daily, and pour it out on the floor of the lifeship!"

He paused, waiting for their reaction, but they were silent.

"All right," he said. "On the other hand, I know the strain you're all under. We need to work together, not fight each other. So I also give you my word as Adelman that if we all—including the Captain—come through this alive to 20B-40, I'll buy up the contract to indent on each one of you and make you a present of it. You'll all be free to build your own estate and pay for your children's education or spend your own earnings in making any life you want. That's a promise, not a bribe. I don't care what you do, as long as you keep yourselves alive and help to keep everyone else alive with you. You've got my word."

H turned and went back to the control section, where Groce still sat. It was surprising that the other had not followed him back to see what the excitement was. Looking at the man, Giles guessed that the shock of Giles' anger had left the little man too frightened to risk doing anything that would push the Adelman over the brink into some action that might destroy Groce completely.

"Back to work," said Giles, briefly, reseating himself in the empty command chair.

They returned to their task. One ship-day went by, then another. . . . Groce dozed between times when Giles wanted him, but Giles kept himself going out of some inner determination he had not known he possessed. He was beyond knowing whether he was or not, now. He hardly knew if he slept or waked. But something kept him moving. Moving slower and slower all the time, but moving . . .

Somehow, they were at last at their goal. A final figure looked up at him from Groce's compute display.

"Is that it, then?" Groce was asking. "The correction factor we need?"

"It could be the correction factor for a course to hell, for all I know." Giles heard his own hoarse voice answering from someplace far off, as if someone else was speaking, distant at the end of a lightless tunnel. He reached out, slowly and carefully, and with fingers that wobbled like those of a drunken man, he punched the correction factor into the course change that was already set up on the lifeship's control panel.

"Now . . ." he said, and thumbed the drive switch.

It was done. There was no sensation of movement or change of direction, but it was done. Clumsily, he got to his feet and stepped out past Groce, away from the control panel.

"You should get some sleep now," Mara said, coming up quietly behind him. She touched her hand to his shoulder, steadying him as he tottered, and unconsciously he covered her fingers with his own hand. Her skin was soft and strangely cool to his touch.

"Yes . . ." he said, still from a long way off. "I guess I need it."

"I'm sorry"—her voice was low in his ear—"I hinted about . . . what you know about, when Biset tried to kill the Captain."

"That's all right," he said. "It doesn't matter."

"It should," she said. She was guiding him to a cot. It was his own cot. The long shape of the Captain lay still on Hem's. He was aware now of Hem standing beside it, watching him. Giles dropped heavily on his cot and lay back.

"A little sleep . . ." he said. "Yes. Just a little . . ."

He went away then, off into the same lightlessness of the long distance where his voice had already preceded him, leaving ship, arbites, and Albenareth Captain all behind.

13

It was the last fruit on the vine.

They were all watching as Giles plucked it and cradled it in his hands. It was full, plump, filled with juice, and it had remained on the vine until the absolute last moment. The juice container was about three-quarters full—about six days' supply on half rations. They had come a long way to this moment when the final fruit was plucked, the last liquid extracted. After this . . . ?

Hem lifted the handle of the press carefully so Giles could place the fruit into the opening. Then the big arbite pushed down, over and over again, until the last drop had been pressed from the pulp and had dripped into the plastic container. It was a pitifully small amount. Giles removed the pulp and divided it into eight equal amounts.

"Eat it all, right away," he said. "There's still water in the pulp, so we'll skip today's juice ration. And from to-morrow on we'll go on half rations until all the juice we have is used up. This is the only way. We have to stretch what we have as long as possible, while there's still hope."

There were no arguments. They choked down the pulp, chewing it to extract every last drop of juice, licking the bowls dry afterward. Giles poured the juice from the last fruit carefully into the tank, then went to make his noon check of their course. He was doing it faster now. Once it had been set into the controls there was little else he could do for six hours. The stars in the screen seemed unchanged,

134

changeless, and he fought hard against a feeling of black despair that threatened to overwhelm him. Mara came up, walking slowly as they all did now, her clothing hanging loose on her thin body. She pointed to the screen.

"Which one is it?" she said. "I don't mean 20B-40 itself. I know we can't see that. I mean 20B-40's sun."

He tapped a spot of light, no different in appearance from so many of the others.

"Shouldn't it be getting larger, or brighter?"

"No. Not until we've made our last warp shift. This screen is for navigation only. In any case a star doesn't look any brighter until the last day or two of flight."

"But we *are* on the right course?" There was need for reassurance in her voice.

"I believe so," he said.

"If it is the right course, then how much longer will it be?"

"According to what the Captain told me, we could be there about ten days from now. But that would be on her course, under ideal conditions. I don't think we can expect that well of my navigation, even if it's right. It could be more than ten days."

"You're not very encouraging," she said, with a weak attempt at a smile.

"Sorry . . ." he said, staring at the controls. His voice ran down and stopped. He could think of nothing more to say.

The conversation died like most of them lately, ran down without any real point or ending. He dozed in the chair and when he opened his eyes she had left. The stars looked very, very cold.

Forty-first day—12:00 hours

The last drop of juice dripped from the faucet into the bowl with a small plopping sound. The very last. There was nothing to be said, so they drank their rations in silence. The last.

There were no buds on the vine, although they kept checking. There were no buds anywhere, and no sign of fruit at all. The *ib* vine seemed healthy enough, covered with a fine crop of glossy, flat leaves. They had tried chewing the leaves, but it was useless, since they were very dry

and bitter and seemed to use more saliva than any amount
of water they might supply.

Forty-second day

Forty-third day

Forty-fourth day

Forty-fifth day

Forty-sixth day

"Do you still keep checking the course?" Mara asked
in a whispered, bitter voice. "You still keep trying?"

"Yes. Have to . . ." Giles whispered back. He was in
no better shape than the others. Thirst, he thought, with
dull-witted humor, was no respecter of class.

"We're going to die, I know that now. Di is in some
kind of a coma, hasn't opened her eyes in a long time. I
think she'll be the first to die. I don't want to die that way,
just giving in. Will you kill me?"

"No." He raised his head. "If anyone lives, we all live."

"You don't want to help me. You want me to suffer."
For the first time her voice was petulant, as if she would
have cried had there been tears to cry with.

He sat in his command chair. The others lay on the
cots or the floor without energy or desire to move. Someone had turned the recorder on and no one had the strength
to turn it off. A girl's reedy voice sang a repetitious song
in which the word "love" seemed to be repeated an unusual
number of times. A drum beat a monotonous rhythm in
the background, and there was too much percussion. It
would have been very annoying to Giles normally; now
he was scarcely aware of it. His throat hurt, his eyes
burned, his body felt completely desiccated; all desires and
sensations fled before the overwhelming thirst. Perhaps
Mara was right: This was not a good way to die. The
singer shrilled, the percussion clanged and banged. The
inner door of the spacelock opened.

Reality had become detached. Hallucination held him,
supplied visions his eyes could not see, swung inward the
door that opened on the spacelock and then into empty

space, and supplied an image of a spindly-legged Albenareth in a spacesuit, removing the helmet.

When a voice behind him screeched, then howled again,
he realized that the others were seeing this hallucination,
too. Perhaps, after all, it was not an hallucination. Gasping,
he pushed himself up on his elbows, climbed to his feet,
holding to the control panel for support, staring. The helmet came off to reveal the wrinkled, dark, seamed face
of an Albenareth, staring at him.

"You did not answer the communications call," an alien
voice buzzed in awkward Basic.

"Water . . ." rasped Giles, in a voice dry as sandpaper.

"I have none. It will be supplied. The communications
—we called."

"Don't know where the comm. controls are, how it
works. *Water!*"

"There is trouble with the *ib* vine?"

Giles dropped to his cot, laughing voicelessly, laughing
uncontrollably, clutching his midriff and rocking back and
forth under the incomprehension of the alien gaze. Water.
Trouble with the *ib* vine! *Water!* All they wanted was
water!

Something clanged heavily against the hull. It was the
forty-sixth and last day.

14

"An incredible story, Adelman," murmured the manager of the 20B-40 Mining Complex. He was a small, pink man, a graduate arbite, obviously, who had risen to this position of authority. And authority it was, Giles had to remind himself. Amos Barsey was the closest thing to a representative of Earth government on the mining world. "May I top that drink for you?"

Giles smiled agreement and extended his tall glass, watching the dark, cold local beer gurgle into it. A beautiful sight. His hand was tanned dark from the long shipdays under the ultraviolet of the lifeship's overhead illumination—tanned, dark, scrawny as a bird's claw clutched around the beaded glass, by contrast with the healthily fleshed fingers of Barsey.

"Thank you," said Giles. "Kind of you."

He drank, feeling the coolness run down his throat.

"It's still a shock," he said, almost dreamily, "to realize it's all over. My navigation was better than I'd hoped. Only, all the time the emergency communications unit was beaming for help in sub-warp, with none of us knowing it."

"It wouldn't have helped, you know," Barsey answered, "if you hadn't been able to bring the lifeship close enough to our solar system so the local Albenareth here could pick up your signal."

Barsey chuckled unexpectedly.

"I've never seen the aliens that disturbed," he said. "They still can't believe you could manage to navigate the lifeship, when their own Captain couldn't."

"It wasn't her fault," said Giles.

"No, I suppose not." Barsey cast an oblique look at Giles from under his plump brows and his tone became somewhat dry and distant. "A page missing . . . and all that. Another mystery. But I suppose the book could have gotten damaged when the spaceliner was destroyed."

"I suppose," said Giles.

"Yes . . ." Barsey swung his float-chair around in mid-air to pick up a slip from his desk. "There was another mystery. Nothing important, of course. That *ib* vine. The Albenareth thought it had been poisoned, but the space-ship repair station here doesn't have the facilities for chemical analysis. They sent a sample of the nutrient fluid over to our lab for analysis. Quite a list of organic compounds in the sludge—none of them anything we'd consider could hurt the plant. Of course, maybe their experts will be able to pick out something harmful. Oh . . . and there was just a trace of something else." His gaze flicked to meet Giles', flickered away again to a far corner of the room. "A human-type drug, filthy stuff called tonk. That could have done the job, our chemist thinks—if there was enough of it, or it was in the nutrient fluid long enough. No way of telling when the contamination occurred, of course. It could have been from any human passenger who used that lifeship as a safe place to store his drug supply, on any of the spaceliner's last fifty trips. And no point in mentioning that to the Albenareth, as I told our chemist. Just cause bad feelings, I should think."

His eyes met Giles'. The slip dangled from two of his fingers.

"No, I shouldn't think there's any point in mentioning it." He dropped the slip into the disposal slot of his desk top. "Merely confuse the issue, since our medical people didn't find any of your arbites with active sign of any tonk addiction when they were examined after they landed."

"No," murmured Giles, "I don't believe you'd find any of them presently addicted."

"Yes," said Barsey. "Well, enough of that. There's another matter. You made quite a point of wanting our medics to return the shipsuit you wore. Here it is."

He reached back to the desk, opened a drawer, and drew out the torn orange shape of Giles' shipsuit.

"Thank you," said Giles. He felt in the pockets of the suit. There were a few small possessions in them, but the extradition paper he had saved from the blazing spaceliner and guarded so long was not there.

"Something missing?" Barsey asked. The manager had been watching.

"Nothing that can't be done without," Giles said, flatly. It was true. The justicar on 20B-40 who had signed the papers had also been the man who was to be Giles' Oca Front contact, once Giles arrived here. But he had memorized the man's name. It was only necessary to contact him and either get a new set of papers, or be directed to Paul's hiding place so that Giles could take care of the assassination here, on 20B-40. Killing Paul on 20B-40 meant certain capture and condemnation for Giles; but, he told himself now, if he was to back off from that now, it would have to be for a better reason than just not wanting to be caught. He had brought the arbites safely to planetfall without loss of a single life, so his good name as a *Steel* in that respect was clean. What happened now, provided it was for the good of the race, should make little difference to him, personally. And the deaths of those who had been trapped in the flaming spaceliner were still a debt on his conscience, waiting to be discharged by the only thing that in decency could do so—an act that would preserve the future for the human race. One that possibly could even aid the future of the Albenareth, as well. The alien crew and officers who had died in the burning ship had died willingly; but still . . . Giles roused to hear the manager speaking to him.

". . . this is a somewhat isolated and lonely world," the manager was saying. "There are no Adelborn here, barring yourself, sir; and the fact that we have to depend on each other a good deal on these Colony Worlds has made us close—even close with the Albenareth who're similarly stationed here. You'll find"—Barsey coughed—"we think a little differently from those back on Earth, arbite and—forgive me—Adelborn alike."

He checked himself.

"Well, well, I didn't mean to rattle on," he continued. "There's a ship calling here in two days, headed back for Earth. I understand you wanted passage on it."

"That's right." Giles got to his feet. "I just have to look

up an old friend. You'd know him, I suppose? He's one of your justicars—Olaf Undstead?"

"Olaf—I'm so sorry!" Barsey scrambled to his own feet, looking unhappy. "He died—just last week. You say he was an old friend?"

"I'd come out here to see him," Giles said.

"What an unfortunate—but let me give you his address." Barsey scribbled on a slip with a stylo. "He had a sort of housekeeper-companion. A free man, former arbite. His name was Willo. Arne Willo."

He passed the slip to Giles, who took it automatically, a cold feeling settling in his chest.

"Yes, thanks," said Giles automatically.

"Arne can tell you all about him," said Barsey. "If there's anything else I can do, come back and see me at once."

"Yes," said Giles. "Yes, I'll see you again before long. . . ."

He turned and went out. Outside the Mining Complex Headquarters, he took a two-man autocar to the address Barsey had printed on the slip.

He had expected to find the address within the domed structure of the Complex itself. The atmosphere of 20B-40 was breathable, but arctic in its temperatures for most of the year—though now, which was during its summer months at the latitude of the Complex, it resembled barren, snowless winter in some area of lava fields and shattered rock. But he discovered that in recent years dwellings had sprung up outside the giant dome of the Complex—either singly or in groups, under small domes of their own. He therefore found himself directed to an exit port, where an attendant sealed him up in a thermal suit, transparent helmet included, and seated him at the controls of a rock buggy, a simple electric-powered, three-wheel vehicle, equipped with an autopilot compute that could be set for the address he wanted.

A second later he was outside the dome, bouncing over the rough rocky surface on the outsize wheels of the buggy. The incredibly distant white dwarf sun of the mining world illuminated the landscape around him no more than the full moon might back on Earth, and with much the same eerie contrast of pale light and black shadow. Behind him the huge Complex dome was like some enormous crouching monster, that dwindled as he moved off from it.

The autopilot of the buggy drove it steadily toward its
as yet invisible destination. Under the dim light of the
dwarf sun, the surface of 20B-40 was like a small, rocky
platform surrounded by uncountable numbers of stars. It
came to Giles, strangely, that after all his days of being
lost in the tiny lifeship, it was now, with his feet firmly
on planetary surface, that the utter, incomprehensible
depths were making their impact upon his feelings. On
the lifeship the stars had been only points of light on a
screen. Here they were naked and real, and seemingly
almost close enough to touch.

Reality, in fact, enclosed him. Even through his thermal
suit, it reached and cooled him like the touch of some
wind that could freeze him to the bone if he dared to
face it without coverings. In the thin light of the far
daystar owning this lifeless world, his beliefs about the
situation of men and Albenareth and all his own personal
plans and duties shrank in his mind's eye to passing things,
inconsequential, transient touches of warmth in a cold
universe. Touches that would come and go, in any case,
leaving no mark or sign of their having been.

In the end, said a deep, atavistic part of him, there's
only survival. Nothing else counts. Nothing else matters.

No, said his stubborn, upper mind. There has to be
meaning. Survival without a meaning to it is nothing.

Survival, said the deep gut part of him, insisting.

Meaning, he said above, in his upper mind.

Surviv—

He wrenched his mind away from the internal argument. The rock buggy was approaching a dome which,
by its size, should house no more than one dwelling. The
buggy trundled forward as if it would smash itself against
the blank-surfaced, back-curving outer wall. But half a
dozen meters from it, the wall opened an iris and the
buggy carried him inside, the iris closing after them.

Within, there was a small garage area large enough to
hold three other rock-buggy vehicles like Giles', but empty
at the moment. He parked his own buggy, got out, and
approached a door in a further wall. There was an an-
nunciator button inside it, and he pushed it, but no one
answered from within the house to ask who had come
calling. He put his hand on the button latch, experimen-
tally, and it gave, unlocked to his touch.

The door opened before him. He stepped through it into a lounge room, wide, white-ceilinged, and filled with comfortable chairs—empty except for one large figure that rose at the sight of him. It was Hem, holding a laser pistol.

15

"Hem!" Giles snapped out the order instinctively. "Don't point that thing at me! Put it down!"

Hem looked puzzled for a moment, then his face creased in contrition.

"Sorry, Honor, sir," he said. He stuck the pistol into the waistband of the gray work slacks he was wearing. Giles drew a deep breath.

"What are you doing here?" Giles demanded.

"I had to stay here," said Hem. He beamed. "To guard you."

"*Guard* me?" Giles felt a cold prickling beneath the back of his collar as sweat popped out there. He had been just about to order Hem to give him the laser. But if Hem had already been given other orders about the weapon, a direct command might not be wise. Giles altered his tactics. "What are you doing here anyway, Hem? Doesn't a man named Arne Willo live here?"

"Oh yes," said Hem, "but he had to go someplace else for a few days."

Giles felt his temper begin to stir. He forced it down. It was not Hem's fault that the big arbite laborer was limited to simple answers to simple questions. There was something going on here; a part of it was that laser in Hem's possession, as dangerous a toy in those big hands as a live grenade would be in the grasp of a five-year-old child. It might be significant that Hem had put the weapon back into his waistband, instead of laying it down out

144

of easy reach as Giles had ordered. Or perhaps it had meant nothing at all. The situation called for a careful phrasing of questions.

"You're here all alone, then, Hem?" Giles asked.

Hem nodded.

"They all went to make sure nobody was after you."

"Who's *they*, Hem?"

"You know, Honor, sir. Everybody. All of us on the ship."

"I see," said Giles. "You mean Mara and Biset, Groce, and the rest?"

Hem nodded again. He seemed to have forgotten the laser at his waist. Giles began to walk slowly toward the massive arbite. If he could get close enough to simply reach out and take the weapon from Hem . . .

"Are they coming back soon, Hem?" he asked, as he moved. If he could keep Hem talking, the bumper would have no attention left over to focus on what else Giles might be trying to do.

Hem nodded.

"Guess what, Honor, sir?" he said.

"Just a moment," said Giles, talking calmly and steadily as he continued to advance, "then I'll guess. First, I want to know how you knew I'd be coming here."

"She knew," Hem said.

"She? You mean Mara?"

Hem shook his head.

"No. Not Mara. The split—Biset."

"So," Giles said. He was only a few casual steps from Hem now. "It was Biset who knew I was coming out here. How did she know?"

Hem shook his head, looking puzzled.

"I don't know, Honor, sir," he said. "She didn't tell us. She just said we all had to come out here, because you'd be coming here sooner or later. Then, when you came in, everybody had better go look and make sure nobody was after you. So, when the light went on for the garage, everybody went out to see. Everybody but me."

Giles checked his forward movement, under an irresistible temptation to turn and see if anyone was behind him. If Biset and the others had just stepped outside the dome enclosing this building for a moment, they might be back inside even now. He risked a quick glance over his shoulder and around the room, but it was still empty and silent, except for Hem and himself.

"Guess what, though, Honor, sir?" Hem was asking again. Giles looked back to see the broad face before him literally glowing with excitement and happiness.

"What?" Giles asked, taking another step forward.

"I'm going home!" Hem almost shouted. "I'm going back—to Earth."

"Going back?"

Surprise checked Giles' feet.

"Going back, you say?" he echoed, slowly.

Hem nodded vigorously.

"I'm going to see Jase!" he said. "And I'm going to say to him, 'Jase, guess where I've been?' and Jase, he'll say, 'Where? They put you in some other barracks?' And I'll say, 'I was clear off Earth. I was out in a spaceship and in a lifeship and on a whole different world. Look, Jase,' I'll say, 'I brought you back a piece of that other world to show you!' See . . ."

Hem fumbled in his slacks pocket and came out with a small bit of igneous rock, obviously picked up somewhere outside the dome.

"And Jase'll say to me, 'Hey! Great you're back!' He'll say, 'I've been waiting for you to get back. That's why I didn't pick some other bumper for a beer-mate.' "

Giles' ears pricked up. Had that been a sound from somewhere in the structure? No, it must have been only his imagination. He turned back to Hem, who was still rehearsing the conversation he would have with Jase when the two were back together again.

"Just a minute, Hem," said Giles, taking advantage of a momentary pause of the other, to draw breath. "What makes you think you're going back to Earth?"

"She said I could," Hem answered, happily.

"She?"

"Biset," said Hem.

"Well, damn her guts!" said Giles, with a sudden spurt of anger. "Hem, listen to me. Biset doesn't have any control over where you're stationed. She can't arrange to have you shipped back to your barracks on Earth."

"Oh yes, sir," said Hem, solemnly. "She's a split. Everybody knows a split can do anything."

"They do, do they?"

"Sure, Honor, sir. They can put you in jail and beat you and keep you there for the rest of your life. Or they can get you transferred anyplace you want if they like you enough. They can even just kill you, and the judges and all say it's all right."

Giles stared at the big man with tightened eyes.

"Hem," he asked, "who's been telling you all this nonsense? The World Police don't beat anyone. That sort of thing hasn't been allowed for a couple of hundred years."

"Oh yes, Honor, sir!" Hem was very earnest. "They don't beat Adelmen, but any arbite who gets in the wrong place or doesn't do what they tell him, they beat him at least a little. Even an office arbite. A couple of them beat our timekeeper once for letting half a dozen barracks gangs of us into town, one day they didn't want any of us there. Of course, with office arbites, they usually just send them to jail or transfer them someplace bad."

"Now listen to me, Hem," said Giles, sternly. "You've been frightened by a lot of tall tales. You don't understand. For anyone in the Police to get away with anything like that nowadays, nearly every other branch of social control—the courts, the records departments, everybody—would have to be involved."

Hem looked unhappy.

"But they do it, Honor, sir," he said. "And they can send you anywhere. She *can* send me back to Earth—Biset!"

Giles recognized a blank wall, and shifted his questioning.

"All right, Hem," he said. "We'll talk about that some other time. Tell me why it is Biset's going to help you get back. Can you tell me that?"

"Yes, sir," said Hem, cheerful again. "She said it'd be all because of you. Because I'd be helping her with you."

"Helping—" began Giles, then stopped. Hem, smiling, had obviously no understanding of what Biset had meant in saying what she had. There was no point in asking the question of him. . . .

A faint sound behind him, as of a foot shuffling on some smooth surface, made the back of his neck chill abruptly. He spun about—and they were all there. Mara, Groce, Esteven, Di and Frenco—and Biset, like Hem, holding a laser pistol. But, unlike Hem, the Policewoman was not holding hers casually.

"Don't move," Biset said. "Don't stir a muscle until I tell you to!"

Her laser was pointed directly at his chest. He stood still—and from behind some drapes at the further end of the room a seventh figure entered. A man, Adelborn, tall and erect, with a thin, handsome face but without the tan normally found on Adelborn features.

"Well, Paul," said Giles.

"Hello, Giles," said Paul Oca, halting beside Biset. "So you tracked me down here, after all?"

"But not for long," said Biset, almost with relish.

"No, not for long." For a second a frown shadowed Paul's face. "Of all the Adelborn in that glorified debating society I founded, Giles, I'd hoped that you'd be the one to see the light. The time for change is here, and nothing can stop it. You remember Tennyson's 'Morte d'Arthur'? 'The old order changeth, yielding place to new . . .'"

"True enough," said Giles. "I believe it. The old order's about to change, Paul, but not necessarily the way you see it changing."

"Oh?" Paul Oca's dark brows raised.

"That's right," said Giles. "For one thing, it's never occurred to anyone to realize that the Albenareth are up against the same problem we are. Only the way they think of death is so alien to the way we think of it that nobody saw the parallel. But we and they can help each other—"

"Giles, Giles," Paul interrupted, shaking his head. "How long are you and the others going to cling to straws, in the hope of getting change without trauma? Change never comes easy. Face it. In this case the price of it is nothing less than amputation of the two useless and crippling elements in our society so that a true middle culture of the human race can take over."

"Amputation?" Giles stared narrowly at him.

Paul nodded at Hem, as someone might nod at a post, or an animal chained to a post. His voice deepened.

"As long as the Adelborn and the genetically suppressed arbites, like this one, still exist, change is blocked. But the human race can't endure that block any longer. We've got to cut loose at any price, and build a strong, new management class out of the best of the arbites, in a culture that's wholly arbite—arbite alone."

"The *best* of the arbites?" Giles looked at him keenly. "Since when were you concerned only with the *best* among the arbites?"

Paul's aristocratic face became even a shade paler.

"Don't chop words with me, Giles," he said. "Obviously some group has to remain in control while the middle culture is maturing."

"What group? And what do you mean by cutting loose at any price? You can't just line up all the Adelborn and work arbites and shoot them down!"

Paul's face did not change. It was like the ice-cold visage of some ancient Roman's marble bust in a winter-frozen garden. The silence that was his answer stretched out in the room.

"By God!" said Giles at last, on an indrawn breath. "You actually are planning it! You're planning to kill millions of people—*millions*—to make this change of yours take place!"

"It's something that has to be done, Giles," said Paul. "That's why we couldn't let you find me. It'll take another six months to set up a world-wide, spontaneous purge of Adelborn and manual arbites alike—"

"Hey," said Hem. His unnaturally old, hoarse voice broke in on Paul's words. "You aren't going to hurt Jase? You aren't going to do that?"

Giles hardly heard Hem's words. He was staring wolfishly at Paul.

"Who's 'we,' Paul?" he asked.

"Listen, Biset," Hem was saying, looking at the Policewoman, "listen, you don't have to send me back to Earth. Just don't hurt Jase."

Biset laughed.

"You don't think it was for your sake you were going back to Earth, did you, bumper?" she said. "No, it's for our sake—because you can be useful that way."

"That way?" echoed Hem, bewilderedly.

"This way," said Biset.

Calmly, she pointed the laser pistol in her hand and pressed the firing button. The pale sighting beam that guided the laser thrust seemed barely to touch Hem's broad chest, but his knees sagged. Slowly, he fell and Biset shot him again in the chest as he was going down.

He had fallen forward. He rolled painfully onto his side to look up at Biset.

"It hurts," he said. "Why—"

There were no more words in him. His eyelids fluttered for a second, then closed, and he lay without moving.

"Why?" Biset told his corpse. "To make sure anybody coming after your high and mighty Adelborn friend here runs up against a dead end."

She turned to face Giles with the laser still in her hand. Suddenly realizing she was about to shoot him also, Giles half crouched to spring. But before he could leap at her, a shocking coldness lanced through his left shoulder and his knees went weak without warning. He caught at the back of a chair and kept himself from falling. Through blurred vision he saw Mara wrenching the weapon from Biset's grasp. Then his vision cleared and he saw Mara clearly, holding the laser, half-pointed at Biset.

"You idiot!" she was raging at the Policewoman. "Didn't I say I had to be the one to shoot him? The wound needed to be placed just right anatomically if he's to live until he's safely away from here. Now you've complicated things!"

Biset's teeth drew back from her lips. She almost snarled like an animal.

"Don't give me orders! You and your handful of Black Thursday fanatics aren't running things. It's the Association that's been preparing for this day for two hundred years—and it's only the Association that's got the size and power to take over, when the change comes. I don't do what *you* say, you bumper's-get; you do what *I* say!"

Giles still held to the back of the chair, although he was already beginning to throw off the effects of the shot. Lasers could be lethal when one of their beams hit a vulnerable spot in the human body, but in a non-vulnerable area they made a particularly clean, self-cauterizing wound that—except for the heat shock when the beam first struck flesh—did less overall damage to the body than many earlier weapons had done. It was a little like being run clear through by a very thin sword blade at forge heat. Biset's shot—as far as Giles could guess—had struck high on his shoulder and gone mainly through flesh and muscle without touching a bone or an important blood vessel. He had been lucky. But it might pay not to act as recovered as he was, just at the moment.

"Association?" Giles said, gazing from his chair at Biset. "What Association?"

Biset laughed at him.

"Fool!" she said. "Overeducated fool! Do you think worldwide revolutions are made by a few philosophers like yourself and your friend there"—she nodded at Paul —"or even by half a hundred like her Black Thursdayites" —she turned toward Mara—"who solemnly go out to get themselves shot down, to provide martyrs for the cause?"

She turned to glare at Mara.

"They couldn't even do that by themselves!" she spat. "We of the Association had to have the proper men in Police uniform, ready and briefed to make sure they were all killed on the spot, neat and tidy, otherwise the whole thing would have come apart."

"All right," Giles said. "Tell me. This Association— what is it?"

"What is it?" Biset said, turning to him. "What do you think it is? An *Association*, a network, of all the arbites who did the real work under you so-called Adelborn. Police, administrative, production, and service personnel of high rank like myself." She interrupted her own tirade. "Did you think I was just an ordinary Policewoman? I'm Deputy Chief of the Investigative Arm, Northeast European Sector. It's me, and a few thousands like me—but thousands controlling thousands apiece—who're the Association, the *real* arbite underground that set out to get rid of you Adelborn almost from the first day you were in power."

She turned her back to speak pointedly to Mara.

"Get busy," she said. "Shoot him—your way. Let's get things moving."

"Just a minute," said Giles. He spoke out of a pure instinct, to play for time that seemed to be running out. His head was whirling with what he had just learned, and certain conclusions of his own that developed inescapably from it. He groped for words that would annoy Biset enough to keep her talking.

"So," he said, to the older arbite woman, "you aren't a convert of Paul's after all. I thought you'd come to believe in him."

Biset took the bait.

"Believe?" She almost spat the words. "In *him*?" The

last word was expelled from her lips as if it had been a poisonous toad. "These other fools may believe in daydreams. I belong to the people who've made things happen —from the beginning when your kind took over! Do you think I'd listen to people like him—or her?"

She glared from Paul to Mara.

"It's not a simple job," she said venomously, "to get rid of millions of people over the face of an entire planet in twelve hours. We need those six more months of quiet— perfect quiet, while things are set up—so that no Adelborn gets curious or alarmed. And *this* fool"—she threw a glance at Paul—"had to go and let your amateur Oca Front sleuths track him down here to 20B-40, in spite of all we could do in the World Police to cover up for him. Whether you killed him or brought him back, there'd be no way to hush up the fact he'd come this far and been given asylum by the aliens and humans here. *That* had to trigger off an investigation by Adelborn in the Police ranks, and our own plans for a tidy elimination would have been turned up, too."

She stopped talking abruptly. Giles spoke quickly.

"So you knew I was headed for 20B-40?" he said. Then he shook his head. "No, of course, you couldn't have known."

"Couldn't?" flared Biset. "Of course we knew. I came on board for the trip particularly to take care of you. I brought these"—she flung her hand out at the other arbites in the room with a sweeping motion—"as a team to help me. A team pulled from the lower ranks of the Association, a team that knew nothing but how to obey orders. . . ."

She paused to look at Mara.

"All but this one. This one I was forced to take to keep the good will of the Black Thursday idiots!"

"That's very interesting," said Giles—and he meant it. "Then just tell me one thing—"

But Biset was through being conned into conversation.

"I'll tell you nothing," she said, turning to Mara. "All right, girl, you've got the weapon. Shoot him, and let's get going!"

Mara lifted her hand holding the gun. Its slim barrel became a tiny ring with a black dot in its center facing Giles. Beyond that ring, Giles could have sworn he saw something in Mara's face that did not match the pointed weapon—something that begged him to understand.

Then there was a little wink of light from the black dot at the center of the metal circle—and darkness came instantly.

He awoke—if it could be called that, because it was a sick and uncertain return to consciousness—and found himself in some small, dimly lighted space with darkness surrounding it. Mara's face was a few inches in front of his own. He was able to recognize it quite clearly, although it went in and out of focus as he watched. He became aware that her hands were doing things to his body—strapping him in, in fact, to the seat of a vehicle—a seat of the rock buggy that had brought him out here.

"What're you doing?" he tried to ask, but the first word that came out was more like a blurred grunt than anything else.

"Hush . . ." Her voice barely breathed in his ear as she worked with her face close to his. "Save your strength. Don't talk. Listen . . . There wasn't any choice. I *had* to shoot you a second time. They think I placed the burn so that you'll die in about fifteen minutes, well before the buggy brings you back on automatic controls to the main Complex. But I didn't angle the shot the way they think. If you can get to a doctor in the next couple of hours, you'll be all right. You must live. You must . . ." Her lips brushed his cheek faintly as she tightened the strap around his shoulder and chest. "It's all I can do. I'm almost as much in Biset's hands as you are. But remember . . . don't do anything until the buggy gets you to the Complex. Then punch the control keys for the nearest hospital. Don't waste time trying to reach the local police. You understand?"

"Yes," he said, or thought he said. But evidently she understood. Her head nodded slightly, and her face moved away from him, out of his field of vision.

He found himself staring through the windshield of the rock buggy, directly at the closed metal doors he had entered earlier, now glinting metallically in the buggy's headlights. After a moment, the doors parted and the buggy jerked into movement. It rolled forward, out of the doors and onto the rocky, lunarlike landscape of 20B-40.

The distant white dwarf sun was high in the sky now, and the jumbled rocky plain before the windshield of the moving buggy was a panorama in black and silver, in which the headlights of the buggy paled almost to invisibility. Over everything rose the dome of the night and the stars, with all other habitations, including the main dome of the Complex, invisible in the further distant darkness, around the horizon. The buggy jolted and swayed as it went, in spite of its excellent suspension, crossing the boulder-studded and uneven ground.

The jolting intruded a slight nausea into the aura of dullness and discomfort that encased Giles like a bottle. He was not conscious of any specific pain, but a sort of general uncomfortableness seemed to have soaked all through him, even into the marrow of his bones. He was dull-minded, weak, and heavy.

It required a great effort, but he finally forced his mind to think about where he was and what was happening to him. The effort itself woke him slightly, perhaps pumping a little adrenaline into his bloodstream. He became more aware, but at the same time his discomfort sharpened. He was conscious of two overlapping areas of heavy painlike pressure, as if a large bruise was being pressed on by some intolerably heavy weight. One of the areas involved his left shoulder, and the other was just above his breastbone. It had been in the shoulder that Biset had shot him, he remembered muzzily. The pain over the breastbone must be where Mara had burned him a second time with the laser.

The *why* of all these things nagged at his dulled mind. Why go to all the trouble of shooting him, just so, and then sending him back to the central Complex in his rock buggy?

He made an effort to sit up, to see what, if anything, had been done to the rock buggy itself—and his right foot caught against something on the floor at his feet. With a second great effort, he pulled himself up to look down at it. The body of Hem lay there, as if it had tumbled from the seat beside him; and the laser handgun was still tucked in the waistband of the gray slacks.

Every moment was like lifting some great weight, but movement was possible. Slowly, in several successive, jerky efforts, Giles managed to bend forward, reach down, and pick up the weapon. He curled his finger around the trigger button and pointed it at the surface of the buggy seat beside him. He pressed the button.

Nothing happened. The weapon's charge was either exhausted or removed. Effortfully, he shoved the useless, but still dangerous-looking weapon inside his jacket and leaned heavily against the backrest of his seat.

He felt exhaustion imprisoning him like soft but massive fetters. The buggy jolted onward, headed toward the main Complex dome, still invisible on the night horizon.

He passed out a second time. . . .

16

He came to, suddenly, choking on the bitter taste of bile in his throat.

He had been sick . . . or rather his body had tried to be sick, but found nothing in his stomach except digestive juices to expel. The raw, searing throat-and-mouth burn of the internal acids had brought him back to himself again.

He felt clearer-headed now. He was aware of his body in a more normal sense, and the pressure areas were beginning to send signals along his nerves in a more normal fashion—not yet as sharp pain, but rather as deep-seated aches. Under the acid taste lingering in his throat, he was conscious of a raging thirst, and his eyes burned and gritted as if he had been staring into dust-filled air, unblinkingly, for some time. Beyond this, however, his mind was newly alert, with the abnormal alertness of someone under a high fever. He looked down at his feet and saw the body of Hem, still there. He looked ahead through the windshield of the moving buggy and saw the tall black semicircle of the main Complex dome, now partially occulting the stars ahead.

Feverishly, with a rush, the whole plan of Biset and her underground arbites tumbled into understanding before him. Barsey knew he had set forth to visit the caretaker of a dead friend's dwelling. Now he would be on record as returning with one of the arbites who had shared his shipwreck—and that arbite shot to death, while he, himself, showed two burns through him and an empty weapon at hand. Plainly, from what Mara had said, he had been intended by Biset to be a corpse like Hem by the time the buggy rolled automatically into its stall at the main Complex.

That meant an investigation by the World Police—the only ones competent to investigate in a case where an Adelman was suspected of something illegal. Biset, herself, as a fellow survivor of the lifeship journey, would be automatically disqualified from investigating. That meant an investigator must be applied for from Earth, must make the trip out and spend days or weeks—weeks, undoubtedly, thought Giles, if the World Police were as infiltrated with Biset's arbite underground Association members as the Policewoman had claimed. Whoever was sent out would almost certainly be a member of that Association and would spin out the investigation as long as the Association needed or wanted it spun out.

That would give the underground the six months Paul and Biset had mentioned, or as much time as it needed to prepare for the wholesale slaughter of the Adelborn and the work arbites.

Giles made himself move. He managed to reach out and switch on the voice control to the autopilot of the rock buggy.

"Change destination," he croaked at it, as the small white light on the panel before him lit up. "Go to . . . the place where the Albenareth are. The alien area in the main Complex. I want to locate an Albenareth Captain. . . ."

For a moment he doubted that his words had conveyed any clear and adequate order to the autopilot. But then, abruptly, the vehicle altered direction. Giles fell back in his seat, panting. There was nothing to do now but wait— and hope that this new destination he had ordered was not too far away in terms of time.

The buggy rocked and jolted along. After a while, he was able to see that they were close to the high metal wall that was the base of the main Complex dome, and running along parallel to it. They would be headed toward a different entrance from the one at which they had originally emerged. After some fifteen minutes, Giles saw such an entrance approaching. But the doors of it did not dilate as they got close, and his buggy went on by. He lapsed into a state that was half doze, half actual unconsciousness.

The buggy stopped with a jerk.

He roused himself and looked around. He was already inside the dome, in a parking area. Some twenty meters from him was a building that seemed to grow out of the dome itself, and in a wall of the building facing him was a transparent section beyond which the head of an Albenareth looked at him. The thin mouth moved, as if speaking.

Belatedly, Giles punched on his intercom.

"Repeat, your business here?" an alien voice was asking in the human tongue. "You have arrived and flashed a recognition signal, but you have not answered my question. What do you want?"

"Sorry . . ." said Giles thickly. "Intercom off. Sorry. I want to . . . I want to meet with the Captain Rayumung again."

"Which Captain Rayumung? We have a number of individuals here of that rank and honor."

"The . . . Captain Rayumung who lost her ship in an explosion . . . who came to this world in a lifeship with a number of humans, of which I . . . am one. I am an Adelman, of *Steel*. She'll know me. Will you call her?"

There was a small pause before the voice spoke again.

"I identify the individual you refer to. She is now Rayumung past-captain. I will try to locate and message her. Will you come inside?"

Giles started to move without thinking, and found the strength was not in him.

"I . . . have to wait out here for her. I'm sorry. Tell her . . . so. I apologize. Ask if she'll come here to me. But hurry."

"All dispatch is always made."

The state of doze-unconsciousness moved back in on Giles as the intercom fell silent. He roused again to the sound of a tapping on the transparent pane to his right, against which his head had been resting.

He straightened up, turned, and looked. An Albenarethian face was staring in at him from just beyond the transparency. Was Hem visible to it, in the shadows at his feet? With a surge of alarm, he fumbled with the latch of the door below the transparency. It opened, and he half fell, half stepped out to face the alien figure beyond.

"*Captain Rayumung?*" he managed, in Albenareth.

The dark eyes looked down into his.

"I am a past-captain now," said an alien voice in human speech. "But I know you, Adelman. What do you want with me?"

Giles leaned back against the body of the rock buggy to keep from falling. His knees were treacherously weak. They would start to shake visibly in a minute. He tried to go on speaking in Albenareth, but the effort was too great.

"I promised you something," he said in his own language. "I promised to tell you who set the bomb that destroyed your ship."

The alien face watched him. The alien voice buzzed its human words.

"That no longer matters. After further consideration I have given up the life I carried. It will be matured and borne by another. So all connections are broken, and it no longer matters how my ship died."

"Doesn't matter . . ." He stared at her, sick with the weakness from his wounds, unable to think how to deal with this new defeat. "You gave up your . . . Why?"

"I had no honor of achievement to pass on. It was you who piloted your humans to safety. Dishonor canceled is no shame, but neither is it of any assistance. It would be good to find and bring justice upon whoever killed my shipmates and my vessel, but it is nothing to do with the life I conceived. I have given that away. Only for the prospect of achieved honor would there be reason in keeping the relationship with my child that is now parted; and where is there any such prospect? For a ship and all who served it are lost, and that is a thing which nothing can change."

"But," said Giles, "if that loss could still lead to some great good for the Albenareth—all the Albenareth—what then?"

"Great good?" The dark eyes watched Giles' face closely. "For all our holy race?"

"Yes," said Giles.

"How could that be? And how could you, being only human, know what would be a great good for the Albenareth?"

"Because in this case it's involved with what has to be great good for humans."

"There can be no such involvement," said the Captain. "In no way are we alike, human."

"Are you sure?" Giles asked. His legs were close to the end of their strength. Imperceptibly, he began to slide down the side of the rock buggy against which he was leaning. The Captain stood silent. "You lived with me—and the other humans—all those days on the lifeship. Are you so sure still that we aren't alike, so sure there's no chance we could have anything in common?"

The tall figure before him blurred.

"Perhaps . . ." said the Captain's voice. Suddenly, two casually powerful hands caught Giles by the shoulders and lifted him, held him up, pressing him against the side of the buggy. "Are you ill?"

"A little . . . hurt," said Giles.

He moved his lips to say more, but there was no strength in him to form words. Dimly, he was aware of the head of the Captain bending forward as she looked past him, into the buggy. This close, she could not miss seeing the body of Hem.

Giles waited for her demands for an explanation, for the alarm that she would now surely give. But nothing of the sort happened. Instead, he felt himself held aside as the door of the buggy was opened, then lifted in, with the body of the Captain hiding the assistance she gave him from the transparent panel where the other member of her race still sat watching.

He was thrust into his seat and the seat clamps folded in automatically to hold him there. The door of the buggy closed. A second later the door on the buggy's other side opened and the tall shape of the Captain moved in to take the seat beside him. She reached for the controls; the buggy moved, pivoted, and drove out through the door in the dome shell where he had entered.

She headed the buggy directly outward from the dome. After a moment, she spoke.

"I am a past-captain," she said. "And I will die now as planet-bound as if I had never known space; nor will there be shipmates who remember me. But there is something here that is unfinished. You defied me to save the last of your slave humans, and here with you is one who is dead and you are clearly more than a little hurt. Also you asked me if perhaps there was not something in common between human and Albenareth after all, and that question troubles me. Before our time on the lifeship I would have had no hesitation in rejecting such an idea. Now, I do not know. . . ."

Her voice died in uncharacteristic fashion. He lay there, letting his body give in to the jolts of the rock buggy.

"Can you speak?" she asked, after a moment.

"Yes," he said. The word came out as a barely audible whisper. He made an effort and strengthened the effort he put into his voice so that it sounded more clearly. "I understand a lot now I didn't before. The Albenareth don't just seek death, any more than we do. Death is only a way station to something bigger—to a racial one-ness with the universe."

"Of course," said the Captain.

"No . . . not 'of course,' " he said. "You don't under-stand how hard a concept that is for humans to under-stand. Death for us is personal and unique—either the end of everything or the freeing of something called a 'soul' that ends up making its own individual terms of unity with the universe."

"The race lives," she said. "The individual is only one of its parts."

"For you Albenareth—not for us. That's the differ-ence," he said. "We think of ourselves always as indivi-duals. 'When I die,' one of us will say, 'the world ends.' You Albenareth can't really appreciate that way of think-ing, any more than we can really appreciate your Portal and your Way."

"Then there is nothing in common, after all."

"Yes, there is," Giles said. "A common lack. Both of our racial philosophies were adequate while each of our races lived only and entirely on the world of its birth. But now we've both gone into space, and it's not enough for you just to translate the Portal and the Way from single-world to universal terms. That way lies stasis and physical death for your race. Likewise, for us humans it's not enough to say merely, 'When I die, the universe ends.' Because now we've seen the universe, and now we know it's too big to vanish just because one individual has died. As individuals we face a universe too big for us."

"A common lack binds nothing."

"But the fact we can help each other binds something —in both our cases," said Giles. The feverish feeling he had experienced earlier had come back on him again, and he was finding a strength to argue that he had not known he had. "What we humans lack can be found in part of what your race already has in its philosophy—an anchor point in the idea that the race survives. As individuals we're too small to face up to the universe, but as a race we can. That is what our philosophy needs. And what you Albenareth lack is the part of what we have—the individual's refusal to give in to a situation where all race teaching says that survival is an impossibility. Remember, *you* gave up; but I brought the lifeship in, after all."

His words echoed and died in the small capsule of the rock buggy, in the face of the unearthly black and silver of the barren nightscape outside the vehicle's windows. He turned his head to stare at the motionless, round, unhuman head of his companion, waiting for her reaction. What it would be he had no way of telling. In human terms he had reminded her most cruelly of her failure in that function of which she had been most proud.

"It is true," the Captain said at last, slowly. "And it is that which has remained unfinished in my mind. You did what you could not possibly do."

"Because I had no choice," he said. "I *had* to get to 20B-40—even if the universe, even if all the Albenareth and all other humans were opposed, or thought it impossible."

The Captain turned her head slowly to look at him.

"But what you describe is anarchy," she said. "No race can live if its individuals are like that."

"Ours does. We live. And here we are—with you Albenareth—in space."

She looked back away from him, out through the windshield at the rocky land.

"Even if you are right," she said, "how could we help each other, your people and mine?"

"I want your aid," Giles said, "to save a human from other humans who would use him as an excuse to destroy many other human lives, millions of lives, in fact. Together we can take him from them, and their excuse as well, as together we brought the lifeship safely to this world. Because, even though you were not able to navigate the ship the last stage of the way, up until that point where I took over, I in my turn would have been unable to navigate. Until then, I hadn't lived through the necessary days aboard that small vessel that were to teach me about your race and mine, and bring me to know how much of what I used to believe was wrong."

"But even if we do something together, what will it prove?"

"It will prove we can supply each other's lack," said Giles. "It can prove we're capable of small things together neither of us could manage alone. To save the lives of some few humans and one Captain Rayumung is not a highly noticeable thing. But to save the lives of many humans, and because of that potentially to save the many lives of the Albenareth, setting them free to follow the Way with new understanding and cooperation with my race—that would be a noticeable thing, something to convince your race and mine that we both need to learn to think differently and work together, in space and on the planets, not just in our own separate spheres. And the benefits from creating that conviction could win great honor for you and your child."

She moved a little in her seat—restlessly, he thought.

"What you talk about," she answered, "goes beyond my personal honor. You ask something unusual from me."

"I know," he said. "If there is a word for it in Albenareth, I have never learned it. But in human the sound is 'friendship.'"

"'Friendship,'" she echoed. "It is a strange word, if it is based on no kinship, no duty association or logical cause for cooperation."

"It is based on mutual respect and a liking," Giles said. "Is that enough? Or not?"

He sat, waiting for her to answer. She turned her face to him again. As always, her eyes and tone of voice were unreadable.

"This is all new to me," she said at last. "It is true I have noticed that among your people and mine on this world of 20B-40—" She broke off abruptly. "Well, in any case what you say is enough for this moment. Where do you want us to go, then?"

The feverish strength drained suddenly from Giles, and he sagged in his seat.

"The rock buggy's log there has the destination point— the one before I came hunting you . . ." he murmured huskily.

Her hand went out to the log control dial and turned

it. Figures flickered to light on the control's small, rectangular screen.

"I have it," she said. "It is now entered in the autopilot."

The rock buggy lurched into a right turn. Giles closed his eyes and let himself float off on the slightly nauseating tide of his weakness. . . .

"We are here," announced the voice of the Captain.

He opened his eyes again and found the buggy standing still, apparently lost in the midst of the white-dwarf-lit plain. Then, slowly, his eyes recognized, ahead through the windshield, the shape of a single-dwelling dome.

"Good," he muttered. "You stopped outside it."

"We had talked of what to do only this far," said the Captain. "You want us to go inside, now?"

"Yes," said Giles. He was coming awake again, drawing on himself once more for the feverish strength that had so far been there for him when he needed it. At the same time, he felt the deep extent of the weakness and pain that were with him now—like a tight metal band enclosing all his upper body.

"Yes," he said again. "But we mustn't drive it. There'll be a foot entrance somewhere, and maybe we can get in without their knowing it."

He made an effort to sit up, but he could move only his arms weakly.

"Wait," said the Captain.

She turned and reached into the back of the buggy, to the compartment in which emergency outside suits were stored. She brought a limp garment forward and held it up—but it was obviously designed only for the smaller shape of a human.

"You can't go out there without a suit," said Giles despairingly within the transparent helmet of his own suit. "It's too cold."

"This vehicle has none other, and this will not fit me," said the Captain indifferently. "It is a short distance and no matter."

She got out, walked around to Giles' side of the vehicle, and opened the door there. Picking up Giles in her arms, she began to walk with him toward the dome. Breath plumed from her lips, and almost at once icicles began to form about her mouth and nose slits. But her arms seemed to hold the weight of Giles' body without effort, and she paced calmly and regularly across the rocky, broken ground.

When she came to the dome, she circled it; and at about eighty degrees from the large doors that had admitted Giles' buggy before, they found a small individual entrance with a latch button beside it glowing with its own internal dim red light to show that it was unlocked. The Captain pressed the button without putting Giles down, and the door slid aside. She carried Giles inside, and the door closed again behind her as a light went on to show them a small entry room, and a further door.

"Can you walk now?" the Captain asked.

Giles shook his head.

"It does not matter," she said. "I will continue, then."

She went forward to the further door, opened it, and mounted a short ramp into the carpeted interior of the house. The sound of voices came to them from along a corridor to their right; and the Captain, turning, carried Giles in that direction until they stepped through the light-curtain obscuring an entrance to find themselves in the lounge room Giles had visited earlier.

She stopped. A reflecting wall across the room gave back her image and Giles'. Inside his suit, he looked pale and ordinary, but the Captain glittered black and silver like the landscape outside, for the fur covering her body was beaded now with tiny crystals of ice where the warm, moist interior air had frozen on contact with her chilled body.

She stepped to a nearby float chair that was empty and set Giles down within it, then unsealed his helmet and removed it. She straightened up again, turning to the people in the lounge, who had been staring at her all this time in silence.

"I bring you the Adelman you know," she said. "He has things he wishes to do—and with my help. But before I help I want to see among you, or between you and him, this thing he calls 'friendship,' which surely all you humans must understand since it is a word of your own language."

17

Seated helpless in the chair, Giles cursed himself. He had, he told himself, made the most basic mistake possible —anthropomorphism. Carried away by his own emotion, he had forgotten that under no circumstances could the Captain have the same human referents for the concept of "friendship" as he, who had tried to bring her to share it with him. What had made him think he could so simply put himself in the mental shoes of a being that was product of an alien physiology, an alien culture?

Biset, Esteven, Groce, Di, Frenco, and even Mara, clustered around the chair in which Paul Oca now sat, stood silent, still staring at Giles and the Captain. But Paul was tied in the chair now, and a thin line of blood had run down from one corner of his mouth. Plainly, Paul had proved recalcitrant in some way, and Biset had turned against him. Perhaps there was hope. Paul had been the closest thing he had ever had to a friend. Perhaps Paul would acknowledge friendship for Giles now and satisfy the Captain. Without the help of the Albenareth, neither he nor Paul had any reason for optimism; and Paul must know that.

"Paul," Giles said swiftly to the other man. "The Captain Rayumung listened to me when I said there was such a thing as 'friendship.' But she has only my word for it. You and I were friends once, Paul. You'll back me up, won't you?"

He threw all the emphasis possible into the last few words, so that Paul should understand the unspoken message. *Back me up and live. Don't, and we're both out of luck.*

Paul stared back at him.

"I—" Paul began, and then his face and body stiffened. Something came into his face and body that Giles had not seen there for years.

"No," said Paul, clearly. "Whatever's to be gained by my agreeing with you, Giles—the answer's no. I've never lied, and I won't lie now. We grew up together, but we were never friends. I had no friends, any more than you did. No true Adelborn feels friendship; only his duty, as he sees it."

His eyes met Giles', without apology. Giles shook his head feebly. With his momentary hope falling in ruins around him, he could not bring himself to blame the other man. Paul Oca, in the end, had answered with the only words his upbringing had left him to say, the sort of words Giles himself had once been ready to live and die by.

"All right," he said. "But if that's all there is to it, Paul, I'm no true Adelborn any longer. Since that lifeship trip I've felt a lot of things that went beyond my duty as I saw it."

He looked at the arbites standing about the chair where Paul sat tied.

"Even with all of you," he said to them. "In the beginning, all I wanted was to come to 20B-40 to find Paul, because that was my duty. I started out in the lifeship determined to keep you all alive because *that* was also my duty—what one of *Steel* should do. But during the trip, I got to know you. I got to like you, all of you, just as persons, in spite of everything each one of you did that disappointed me, jarred on me, or rubbed my temper thin. You aren't angels. No humans ever are. You aren't even Adelborn. But you're the people I lived and nearly died with and you've come to mean something to me now. You—and all the arbites like you, back on Earth."

He gazed at them, a little sadly.

"Doesn't even one of you know what I'm talking about?" he said. "Isn't there one of you who felt it, too—that something I'm talking about?"

Mara suddenly broke from the group and ran to him.

"Get her back here!" snarled Biset. "Esteven, Groce— drag her back here!"

The two men hesitated, turning to stare at each other.

"Go on!" blazed Biset. "Do what I tell you!"

The men turned away from each other. Together they went forward to where Giles sat. But when they reached the chair, they did not touch Mara, who was now standing behind it with her arms around Giles. Instead they turned, one on each side of Mara, and stood facing Biset.

"What's the matter, you idiots?" raged Biset. "Bring her back here!"

"No," said Esteven.

The entertaincom's face was pale, and sweat was rolling down it. But his lips were tight together.

"You don't own me!" Esteven said to Biset. "If it was up to you I'd be crazy or dead, from the tonk. He saved me from the Captain. He saved me from the stuff! Why should I do what you want?"

"That's right," said Groce, hoarsely. "You don't own us."

"Don't own you—why, you bumper-gets—" Biset broke off, for the others who had been standing beside her were now in motion, crossing over to join Mara, Esteven, and Groce beside Giles. *Come back here, all of you!*

Di, alone, hesitated at the sound of the Policewoman's voice. But Frenco caught her hand and pulled her along with him. They reached Giles and turned to face Biset.

"No one owns us," Esteven said to her. "It's different out here on the Colony Worlds. You can't have us beaten up or judged criminals and put to forced labor, here, just because you want to. Here, you've got to prove we've done something wrong."

"You think so," said Biset, grimly.

She reached into a pocket of her suit and came out with her laser hand weapon.

"I can kill you all," she said, harshly, "and claim you're a Black Thursday group. I may be held under house arrest until an investigator comes from the World Police on Earth to check the matter; but when the investigator comes, I'll be cleared—by him or her, whoever they send. Think of that as you're lying in your graves—"

But she had been concentrating wholly on those who defied her. The Captain was suddenly in motion, moving toward her with great strides. Biset jerked the laser weapon about, to aim it at point-blank range at the towering figure.

"Get back!" she shouted. "I'll kill you, too, if I have to."

But the Captain came on. At this range Biset could not miss. Desperately, Giles reached into his jacket, snatched out the empty laser he had found in the rock buggy, and pointed it at her.

"Biset!" he cried.

She glanced at him for a moment, saw the laser, and pulled her own weapon about to shoot him before turning its beam on the Captain. But time was too short for both actions. Giles saw the wink of light at the end of the barrel of Biset's weapon, heard Groce grunt and clap a hand to a burned forearm, then the tall, dark figure of the Captain closed with the slighter human shape before her, and Biset went down. . . .

Giles blinked about him, slumping in his chair. A wave of weakness and dizziness had threatened to carry him off. Now it was clearing, but his eyes were still playing tricks on him. He was seeing double—no, triple—images of the Captain. He blinked and stared again, but they remained. The room was full of Albenareth, and there were other humans there who had not been present a moment or two before. One of them was Amos Barsey, now supervising the release of Paul Oca from his bonds by a couple of men with police armbands—clearly members of the local 20B-40 constabulary.

Freed and on his feet, Paul was led out of the room. As he went, he passed by the chair where Giles still sat, and paused.

"Remember today, Giles," he said, coldly. "Today, you've kept the human race from saving itself and put it on the same road to eventual death that these Albenareth are already on."

"Or perhaps on a new road for both races that's the road to life," answered Giles. "We'll have to wait and see, won't we, Paul? But I'm betting my way's the right one."

Paul turned without a word and let himself be escorted off. Two men carried out the body of Biset, and the space where Paul had stood was occupied a moment later by a man with a medical kit, who began to fuss with Giles' burns. Above the head of the working medician, Giles saw the tall shape of an Albenareth step into view and look down at him.

"Captain?" said Giles in Basic, uncertainly. Even after all those days on the lifeship, he could not be sure to tell the one Albenareth he knew from those he did not know.

"I am satisfied," said the Captain. "It is apparently a real thing, this 'friendship.' There are others of our holy race who have been on such new worlds as this and had experiences with humans that suggest it is not uncommon—I am now told."

"Told . . ." said Giles. He looked about the room, at the other tall, dark shapes. "Where did they all come from?"

"I do not know," said the Captain. "But evidently, while you waited for me, you by your stillness and other unusual behavior aroused a concern in the mind of him of our race who greeted you and sent for me. As a precaution, the local human police were contacted, and these ordered a listening device attached to your rock buggy, while you were unnoticing. We were listened to as we talked and followed here, by both my people and yours."

Giles shook his head feebly. The medician had just given him some kind of an injection and he was feeling the pain recede as strength returned, but he was still far from being himself.

"I don't understand," he said.

"We have been a subject of the attention of both our peoples, here on 20B-40, ever since we landed, Adelman," the Captain said. "As I may have said, our races on these new worlds seem closer to each other than in other places. But I wait for what you promised me."

"Promised?"

"You promised to tell me who it was among you humans who destroyed my ship. I wait to hear, now."

"Giles . . ." It was Mara, speaking beside him, warningly. He put up a hand to calm her.

"I'll tell you," he said.

"Giles!"

"No . . . no. It's all right," he said aside to her. "Listen . . ."

He turned back to the Captain.

"I set a bomb aboard your ship," he said.

"You?" The Captain's tall body moved almost imperceptibly toward him.

"Yes," Giles said. "It was part of a plan worked out by the Oca Front to get me to 20B-40 without arousing any suspicion on Paul Oca's part that one of us had been sent to kill him." Giles shook his head briefly. "To think I left Earth intending to kill . . . but I was wrong about a good many things, then."

He looked back up at the Captain.

"The idea was that the bomb would damage your vessel enough so that you'd want to turn aside to 20B-40 for repairs. Once we'd landed here, I could leave the ship and find Paul."

"I am listening." The Captain's voice was expressionless, remote.

"To make the plan work," said Giles, wearily, "I had to set the bomb off at just the right time. Which was why I knew something about your course and the location of 20B-40 from the position at which the explosion occurred. Also—we thought—the bomb had to be just the right size so that the ship would be damaged enough to make you turn aside from your original course, but not damaged so much that it couldn't make it safely to 20B-40. There was no plan for me to make the trip here in a lifeship."

His voice was harsh as he ended.

"You planned," said the Captain. "But the bomb was larger than you thought?"

Giles shook his head.

"It was the right size," he said. "But it had help we hadn't counted on. Someone else wired another bomb to it—a much more powerful bomb, that couldn't fail to wreck your ship completely." His voice took on an edge. "Good God, where would a bunch of amateur revolutionists like us get hold of something that would make metal burn like dry leaves?"

"Why," asked the Captain, "this second bomb?"

"Because there was another plan I didn't know anything about. It called for me to get to 20B-40 in a lifeship, as we did. But not just me alone, but with a handful of people." Giles lifted a heavy hand to indicate Mara and the other arbites from the lifeship who still stood around his chair. "It was understood that if the ship died, you Albenareth would choose to die with her—all but one of you, who'd pilot the lifeship to safety, out of duty to save the few humans that remained."

"Why did you agree to this second bomb, this further plan?" demanded the emotionless voice of the Captain.

"I didn't. Neither did any of the others on the lifeship, but one. That one identified herself when I first came to this dome here. Biset."

"The female I just killed?" said the Captain.

Giles nodded.

"Biset admitted she'd planned to bring these others, and herself, with me to 20B-40 in the lifeship. By admitting that, she gave herself away. The only way she could have been sure of doing what she planned was if she set the second bomb herself—and made sure it was a bomb large enough not only to destroy the ship, but to make sure no other arbites, except those she'd chosen back on Earth, lived to escape. I'll bet if it'd been possible to examine your ship before the bomb went off, we'd have found every lifeship but the one we took was sabotaged, made unusable."

There was a long silence in the room. Finally, the Captain spoke.

"How could she know that I"—the alien voice broke, uncharacteristically, then went on as unemotional as ever —"that *you* would be able to take command of the vessel and bring it to 20B-40, rather than Belben?"

"She didn't," said Giles. "She and her people were as ignorant as I was of Albenareth ways of thinking. It never occurred to her, any more than it did to me, that you'd do anything but head for the nearest safe planetfall, which was 20B-40. But when you insisted on going on to Belben instead, even if we all arrived dead, she was forced into using the joker in her deck—the one person she'd included just in case there was some dirty work to be done."

He turned his head to look at Esteven.

"She supplied you not only with tonk but with paper to take with it, to begin with, didn't she?" Giles said. "Then she claimed she was out of paper."

"And I believed her!" Esteven's face twisted. "I *believed* her! That's why I went for the book."

"Yes," said Giles. He looked back at the Captain. "So now you know, Rayumung."

"Yes," said the Albenareth. Her head lifted. "And now that I know, I shall take back the child that is mine, and live. For I have canceled my dishonor by slaying the one who slew my ship; and there is also honor to be acquired in this thing you have given me, called 'friendship,' as I shall explain it to others of my holy race."

"Yes," said Giles. "And when you've done that, there's another word you can introduce them to. It's called 'co-operation'—and it can mean human and Albenareth as shipmates working vessels through space together."

The dark eyes glittered on him.

"You have done much, Adelman," said the Captain, grimly. "Be warned. Do not try for too much, too soon."

The eyes were steady on Giles. Slowly, Giles nodded. "Perhaps you're right," he said. "Good luck, anyway, Rayumung."

"The holy race does not proceed by luck," said the Captain. "But by understanding of the Way, on which all things may journey."

She turned away. But just before going she turned back.

"All things but slaves," she said. "However, I find that I have changed my thought about these others here." Her gaze swept over the arbites about Giles. "They have proved themselves not slaves, all save the one I have just slain. This, therefore, is the greater message I carry to the Albenareth, and 'friendship' is the lesser. For in truth, respect between us and you must come before all other things."

She turned and went, erect, unyielding, stalking from their presence with great and measured strides, like someone who now saw her way clear to the uttermost reaches of eternity.